Michel Bernanos was the second of seven children of Georges Bernanos, author of *Diary of a Country Priest* and *A Diary of My Times*. As a young man Michel served in the Free French Naval Forces and soon after World War II he moved to Brazil. He returned to France upon his father's death in 1948 and began writing, first magazine articles, then thrillers and a novel of adventure. But this posthumous book, published in France under the title *La Montagne Morte de la Vie*, was the first work to which he signed his real name. Michel Bernanos was barely forty at the time of his death in 1964.

The
Other
Side
of
the
Mountain

The Other Side of the Mountain

By *Michel Bernanos*

Translated by *Elaine P. Halperin*

Houghton Mifflin Company · *Boston*

1968

First Printing   W

Copyright © 1968
by Jean-Jacques Pauvert, éditeur
All rights reserved. No part of this work
may be reproduced or transmitted in any
form by any means, electronic or me-
chanical, including photocopying and re-
cording, or by any information storage
or retrieval system, without permission
in writing from the publisher. Library
of Congress Catalog Card Number: 68–
29550. Printed in the United States of
America. First published in the French
language under the title La Montagne
morte de la vie *by Jean-Jacques*
Pauvert, éditeur, 8, rue de Nesle,
Paris VIe. Copyright © 1967
Jean-Jacques Pauvert, éditeur.

To Maria Mauban

For truly, Lord, this is the best proof
We can give You of our dignity —
This tide of tears that flows timelessly
Only to expire on the shores of Your eternity!

Charles Baudelaire

Part One

Part One.

Chapter 1

I HAD JUST TURNED EIGHTEEN when, after an evening of drinking, I was persuaded by a friend to sign on board a galleon for one year.

My memory of what proved to be the beginning of an appalling adventure is very vague, almost nonexistent. In truth, not until the following morning was I once again fully in touch with reality. Great was my surprise to find myself stretched out on bare boards and greeted by the intense blue of the sky. Then I noticed the sails, inflated by a gentle breeze, and the white specks of a sea rolling in endless waves to the very edge of the horizon. My astonishment grew as I looked about and saw heaps of coiled rope such as I had seen so often on the decks of ships in port. There was a strong smell of tar everywhere.

I heard steps and immediately closed my eyes again, pretending sleep. This did not save me from the hard thrust of a foot in my side.

"Get a move on, cabin boy," a voice barked. "We've

got to clean the quarterdeck. And move faster than that if you don't want to be hanged from the boom." Another kick accompanied these remarks.

I stood up, staggering a little on the uneven deck.

"Get a move on, I tell you," the voice continued. "Go see the cook. He's waiting for you to help with the grub."

Not knowing where the galley was, I started to wander from the quarterdeck to the forecastle. The wind had risen and the sails, filling with the new air, puffed out their big white bellies. The galleon — I learned its name later — listed to one side and glided over the water like a caress. Its masts creaked in an effort to stand firm before the wind. I met several members of the crew. There was nothing heartening about their expressions, but the fact that they seemed to pay no attention to me was reassuring. I quickly changed my mind, however, upon finding myself face-to-face with the man who had so roughly aroused me. His dark, almost black face grimaced horribly and he said to me in a crusty voice:

"So you refuse to obey, eh? Well, we'll show you! Over here, men," he shouted to the other sailors. "Bring two towropes. We'll have some fun!"

And staring at me with hate-filled eyes, he repeated:

"So you refuse to obey, eh! Well, I'll teach you to be a sailor!"

As if in a bad dream, I watched the crew surround me. An evil, silent laugh on the hard faces of these men made me lose all hope of their taking pity on me.

"Well, man." My torturer, whom I guessed to be the boatswain, began to shout again: "Are the two ropes coming?"

"Yes, here we are, they're coming," a voice answered.

And a young sailor appeared, holding a long rope at the end of which hung a weight.

"Go ahead, tie him to it," the boatswain ordered, pointing me out with a nod of the head.

The sailor looked at me, hesitated a moment, then objected:

"He's only a boy. You think he can stand it?"

"Do what you're told and shut it," was the curt reply.

"All right, all right," said the sailor. "I was only saying . . ."

And without further ado he began to put the rope around my waist. Another sailor approached with a second towrope. The boatswain motioned to him and together they moved toward the front of the ship. I watched them anxiously. One stood at the starboard, the other at the port side, and they passed the rope over the prow, then let it slowly slip under the ship's hull. Now they were coming back toward me. The sailor took the end of the rope he was holding and tied it firmly to the rope already around my waist. Thus I found myself between the two joined ropes. Filled with panic, I glanced beseechingly about me; although I noticed pity on a few faces, a look of sadistic pleasure appeared on most.

Indifferent to these preparations, the blue, fleecy sea

gave forth from the crest of its billows a white foam as light as lace, while the topmast, all its sails flying, seemed gently to stroke the color-streaked sky.

"Come on, throw him over," howled my persecutor.

Several heavy hands seized me and coarse laughter erupted as I was handed over the side. Crazed with terror, I closed my eyes and stiffened as I awaited the shock of the cold water. But I had not reckoned with the cruel refinement of my tormentors. They lowered me as slowly as possible into the watery abyss. I tried to hold myself back by grasping the wooden, seaworn hull, but I merely succeeded in tearing my fingers badly. The men's laughter reached me, mingling with the noise of the rolling sea so close to me. My feet suddenly touched water. And to my surprise, at that very moment I was suddenly filled with a curious composure. I knew that at all costs I must avoid breathing once I was completely submerged. And so I waited to the very last, until the water reached my chin, in order to inhale as much air as possible and to hold back my breath. But, in spite of my precautions, I felt my chest contract atrociously. I was now being dragged to the other side, just as slowly as when I was lowered into the water. I could no longer endure it. I had to have air. I opened my eyes in the hope of seeing the liberating daylight above me. But what greeted me was a terrible vision that made me forget the burning contact with salt. I found I was still beneath the hull. In the greenish, unreal light of underwater places, the ship resembled an enormous dark monster. At that moment I must have fainted because I have no recollection of what happened next. Only afterward did I learn that the captain, attracted by the commotion his crew was making on the deck, arrived on the scene and, realizing immediately what was happening, gave the order to bring me up. Had he not intervened I probably would have perished.

I was stretched out on a hammock that swung to the rhythm of the rolling sea. I could see the horizon through a porthole. It would sink into the sea and surface again with each movement of the galleon. This reminded me of my terrible ordeal and, either from fear or exhaustion, I again lost consciousness.

Harsh sounds reached me. I opened my eyes. It was night. Not far from me a storm lamp was swinging back and forth. The wrinkled face bending over me reminded me instantly of those apples my mother used to set out on the kitchen hearth. The man stared at me with small, black eyes that had no kindness in them but were without malice. He was chewing a quid of tobacco that made his breath smell foul.

"Well, so you're waking up at last, boy? Come on, get up! Mustn't keep your belly empty too long."

"How long have I been sleeping, sir?" I asked him.

"Three days, my boy. And better remember there's no such thing as 'sir' around here. I'm old Toine, the cook. And I need a helper, so I'll take you on, if that suits you. I'm not kind but I'm not hardhearted, either.

And you'll always get enough to eat at this job. Eating's the main thing in life."

"But where are we going?" I asked.

"What? You don't know? You must have filled out a contract in good and proper form, no?"

Wagging his head, he continued: "We're going to look for gold in Peru for the Spaniards, if the English or the Dutch don't sink us first, of course."

"So, we're pirates?" I asked, suddenly interested.

"No, no, we're just chartered," he answered, shrugging his shoulders.

Then, seeing by my puzzled look that I did not understand, he spat out a long jet of blackish saliva and, shifting his quid to the other cheek, said in a gruff voice:

"Come on and eat. You look like death."

I got up painfully. Everything was spinning around me but I managed nonetheless to follow my new boss to the place that served as a kitchen.

It was filthy. Cockroaches three times larger than any I had ever seen were running around among sacks of flour and sugar. Old Toine served me a vegetable soup that tasted delicious from the first spoonful. He watched me eat with a satisfied look. He must have loved his cooking and liked seeing others enjoy it. When I had finished, he said:

"Go get your hammock. You're going to sleep with me in the galley. You'll be better off here than with those swine."

Chapter 2

A FORTNIGHT had passed since we set sail. At first the crew continued to bully me, but each time, pretending he needed me in the galley, Toine intervened, even going so far as to brandish a large butcher knife under the noses of the men.

Early in the morning I would settle down on the deck to peel potatoes. Often I caught myself dreaming as I looked out on the blue infinity. The dolphins, breaking the surface of the water, frequently interrupted my reverie. They rose in the air, suspended momentarily, then fell back gracefully into the liquid elements. The ship itself, its sails spread and its bowsprit seeming to pierce the horizon, gave me the feeling it should be able to fly. As the day advanced, the hot sun flooded the decks with gold. The gentle wind reminded me of my mother's caresses when I was little. When night fell and my work was done, I kept coming back up on deck. I liked to watch the galleon cleave the phosphorescent waters,

making sprays of tiny drops full of minuscle rain-
bows. I also liked to spot the new stars that would rise
up in the horizon to settle in the dark arched vault, under the still watches of the Great Bear.

Gradually, in the presence of all these wonders I was
discovering, my fears and regrets disappeared. I was
even surprised to find that I could hold my own with the
members of the crew. The voyage really seemed to be
off to a peaceful start. One morning, however, we
awoke to an unusual silence. Toine jumped out of his
hammock like a madman, shouting:

"It stopped, the bastard!"

Then, seeing me propped up on my elbow, looking at
him questioningly, he began to scream:

"Do you hear anything? Tell me, do you?"

"No, no," I said, completely bewildered. "No, I don't
hear a thing."

"That's just the trouble, imbecile. The wind has
stopped blowing in the middle of the equator in this
bitch of a spot where there's no current. It can last like
this for days and days!"

He went out quickly. I jumped down from my hammock and followed him. Outside, the large sails, completely deflated, hung down, a sorry, desolate spectacle. The rays of the sun which were slowly spreading
on the horizon were reflected in the sea like an immense
lake of sleeping waters. Already the heat was scarcely
bearable. Members of the crew were performing their
chores in unaccustomed silence.

Toine sent a long spray of spittle over the side:

10

"Take a look at that, boy," he said. "Life itself seems to be hanging in midair. Let's hope it won't last," and he clenched his teeth, "or it'll be hell!"

"Pull in the sails, you bunch of good-for-nothings!" yelled the captain, coming down from the bridge.

For eight interminable days we waited for the wind to return. Steadily, the crisis mounted. First water was rationed, then food. But this proved a mistake because the food spoiled quickly in the extreme heat that assailed the ship from all sides. We had to resign ourselves to getting rid of it by throwing it overboard. Scurvy was not long in showing up. The men's lips and gums took on an ebony cast and swelled to double their normal size. To relieve the suffering of these poor souls, rum was distributed; but more and more was needed, and in the end this was becoming dangerous since it was intended to barter the contents of the hold to obtain a better price for gold.

After forty days of immobility, the potatoes, the only food that had survived the disaster, began to sprout and a frightful odor escaped from the hold that contained them. It was this odor that finally made the captain decide to throw the precious vegetables overboard. This time, however, he met with the opposition of some of the crew. Nothing could make these men, who had become menacing, listen to reason. They claimed that rotting food was better than no food at all. Tired of arguing, the captain handed over the potatoes. The men ate them as they were, without even bothering to cook them, so tortured were they by hunger. A few hours later, suffering atrociously, they died as their horrified companions looked on; no one uttered a word of protest when the last sack of potatoes was thrown into the sea.

In the meantime, Toine and I fed on a small supply of flour meal that he had put aside. I was ashamed of this, but Toine maintained that our entire hoard would not provide a single meal for all the men.

"Besides," he added, "do you think for a minute that if one of those good-for-nothings had any food he'd raise a finger to save his best friend from dying before his very eyes? You forget quickly, lad. It's these same fellows who never once hesitated to give you a bath that almost killed you."

It was this last argument, I must admit, that overcame my remorse. Actually, that was all I needed. Man is above all a coward, often intent only on finding an excuse for his cowardice.

We had now been becalmed for fifty-five days. For three days there had been neither water nor food. Tortured by hunger and thirst, the men had a crazed look in their eyes. The captain had taken the precaution of reinforcing the boards of the rum hold. But one night we were suddenly awakened by a frightful racket. Armed with axes, the men were forcing their way into this hold in spite of the captain's screams as he tried to prevent them. And soon, judging by their shouts of joy,

12

we could tell they had succeeded. We no longer heard the captain's voice. He had probably returned to his cabin. After a moment the men were back on deck and Toine and I could see them through the galley port-hole. They were in a state of total inebriation. In their weakened condition it had not taken them long to get drunk. What a weird spectacle, in the light of the storm lamps: faces with eyes so deeply sunken that they looked like holes, mouths made shapeless by mon-strously swollen lips! Most of these poor devils had already lost their teeth. So thin were they, that one won-dered where they got the strength to create such tur-moil.

At the moment they were sitting around in groups. The boatswain was among them but his condition seemed almost normal.

"That bastard," Toine said, pointing to him, "natu-rally put some provisions aside for himself."

I could not help smiling at the cook's indignation. Hadn't he done the same?

We decided at last to return to our hammocks. A couple of hours passed and still we could not go back to sleep. The heat was stifling and, to make matters worse, Toine had barricaded all the doors.

For a while I had the feeling that something new was happening on the deck. Shouts had replaced obscene songs. I was not mistaken. Toine said to me sud-denly:

"Don't go to sleep, lad, there's going to be trouble. They're all jawing at each other. Soon they'll start scrapping. And on top of it all, that bitch of a wind just doesn't seem to be coming."

At that moment there was a terrible outcry. We rushed to our portholes and what we saw was a nightmarish scene. In a frenzy at the prospect of dying, several men stood face-to-face, their knives in their hands. Although barely able to stand on their feet, they were trying clumsily to throttle each other. Brutalized by their ordeal, they now had no thought save to kill. Horrified at first, I was enthralled in the end by these struggles. Yes, to my great shame, these incipient murderers fascinated me.

They stopped for a moment when the captain appeared, armed with two pistols. But the quiet proved short-lived. A skillfully thrown cutlass struck his throat. Blood spurted out. The poor man staggered, then fell as he fired both his pistols in the direction of the mutineers. One of them, hit by a bullet, fell to the ground holding his stomach.

Wild with fury at the sight of blood, the men seized the captain and were about to throw him overboard when a voice shouted: "Why not eat him?"

A murmur arose, followed by a long silence. Then all the men rushed toward the captain's corpse and it was dismembered in no time at all. Struck with horror, I could not take my eyes off the incredible spectacle. On the verge of nausea, I watched these supposedly civilized beings share the cadaver of their captain. They were eating him now with an ignoble pleasure in which nothing human remained. Some of them, their

14

appetites sharpened by this atrocious meal and feeling perhaps that their hunger was not yet appeased, turned toward the wounded sailor.

"No!" he screamed. But he was killed off savagely and his dismembered body was likewise shared.

Haunted by this horrifying spectacle, I did not go to bed most of that night. Toine lay down on his hammock without a word, but he did not sleep. When I turned I could see him steadying himself by bracing his foot on the rounded wall of the ship. From time to time he raised himself up to eject a long stream of spittle. The heat had become so unbearable that I asked:

"What about opening the portholes a bit?"

"You may," he answered, "the dogs have gorged themselves."

I hastened to leave the narrow apertures ajar. But I was immediately seized with a fit of vomiting. A sickening, sweetish odor had invaded our private kitchen, where no fresh air had entered.

"It stinks of blood, lad," Toine said. "If you can't stand it, better close things up."

I acquiesced. But before returning to my hammock I cast a last glance outside. The night was about to draw to a close, making the stars look pale. The skyline, where the day was beginning, was streaked with gold. The men, now silent, were for the most part stretched out on the deck, digesting their crimes. Some stared straight ahead with haggard, empty eyes as if they were seeking oblivion in the distance where the unsullied day punctuated the dawn.

15

Chapter 3

I AWOKE late in the morning, around noon. The heat
was overpowering. The atrocious scenes of a few hours
earlier immediately sprang to mind and at once I sank
into profound despair. Would it soon be my turn? Was
there any way out of this hideous situation? I must
have sighed, for Toine's voice quickly made itself
heard:

"Well, lad, there you are. Are you waking up?"

He was standing near the porthole. I walked over to
him and, full of apprehension, ventured a look outside.

The macabre remains that still littered the deck —
shreds of flesh stuck to their bony substance — had
turned blackish as a result of the heat. And — endless,
repetitive mystery — a green fly was already buzzing
around eagerly. The men had gone back to drinking
rum, doubtless in the absurd hope of quenching their
thirst. But now they could bear it no longer and we saw
them, their insides on fire, shrieking like animals and
writhing in pain, their hands clenched over their bel-

lies. Several of them, no longer able to withstand the agony, toppled overboard in the immensity of the undrinkable water.

Toine touched my shoulder. "You see, lad, it's not a pretty sight when men go mad. Worse than mad dogs."

"What will the others do?" I asked, my voice trembling.

"Bah, they've tasted blood. When they get hungry again they'll start all over and eat each other. Unless that bitch of a wind starts to blow!"

At that very moment the rolling pin on the kitchen table began to move. Toine grasped my arm abruptly.

"Did you see, lad, did you see?"

And, since I did not seem to understand the importance he attributed to this, he continued joyously:

"The current! Hear it? The current! That's the wind coming! By tomorrow it'll be blowing."

God be praised! We were reaching the end of our terrible nightmare. I could hardly believe it.

And all of a sudden my joy exploded. I began to laugh and cry at the same time. Toine looked at me, nodding; he seemed almost moved. Finally he said:

"Better not rejoice too soon, my boy; our troubles are not yet entirely over."

"But who will command the ship, now?" I asked.

"Fear," he answered, and a long shiver went up and down my spine.

*

17

A few hours later Toine and I were still locked in our galley. The heat had driven the crew, or what was left of it, from the deck.

"I can't stand it any longer," Toine said suddenly. "I'm going out to splash some water over that damned deck."

Before unlocking the door, he took the precaution of slipping a pistol into his belt along with his knife. I was about to follow him.

"No, lad," he said, "better stay here."

But seeing that I had no intention of doing so, he shrugged his shoulders and said laconically as he handed me a pistol:

"Then take this."

The sun was beating down on the deck, which was like a furnace when we stepped out. Our feet were literally scorched. We each took a wooden bucket, attached a rope to it and began to draw sea water, which we threw over the blood stains that had turned brown. I left to Toine the task of throwing the remains overboard. Nothing in the world would have induced me to touch them. A goodly portion of the deck had been cleared when a sailor suddenly sprang from the shadow of a hatchway and yelled:

"Leave that alone, it's mine. That's my food! D'ye hear? Leave it!"

At the same time he brandished an iron whelp. It seemed plain that he was about to crack Toine's skull. Taken by surprise, Toine had no time to reach for his weapons. I did not hesitate. Drawing my pistol from

18

my belt, I fired on the madman, not even taking time to aim. The sailor fell, a gaping hole in his forehead. Stupefied, I looked at him sprawled at my feet. Suddenly I began to tremble like a leaf.

"Come, come, lad," Toine said, tapping me on the shoulder. "It was his life or mine. He'd have had me for his next meal if it hadn't been for you."

He leaned over the sailor to make sure he was really dead. Then, grasping me by the shoulder, he said:

"Come on, help me. We'll throw him into the sea before the others take it into their heads to eat him."

I seized my victim by the legs, not without repugnance, and we swung the corpse into the water. A good number of sharks, attracted for some time by the smell of blood, had surrounded the boat. They lunged at this unhoped-for prey and divided it up in a disgusting fashion.

We went back to the galley in silence. It was almost cool inside after the extreme heat of the deck. We drank a little water, noting as we did so that our provisions were dwindling rapidly. Then we ate a little flour meal which Toine had moistened earlier to give it consistency. Neither the terrible odor that emanated from it nor its abominable mildewed taste bothered us, so overpowering was our hunger. Nevertheless, I realized later that I could not continue much longer to abuse my stomach in this way.

Needless to say, as soon as we returned to the galley Toine again locked the door. At any moment we might be attacked. Fortunately we had an ample supply of gunpowder and bullets. There was nothing more to do but wait. We stretched out on our hammocks.

Imperceptibly, as time passed, the ship began to move. I finally fell asleep.

Songs and screams from the deck woke me. Night had fallen. They're starting up again, I thought anxiously. I raised myself a little and saw Toine standing in front of the porthole. He had not lit the lamp, probably to avoid attracting attention.

"What's happening?" I asked.

"Those imbeciles are starting on the rum all over again. If only, instead of swilling their heads off, they had had the good idea to hoist the sails, we'd be moving."

I got up and peered through the other porthole. The few remaining survivors were seated around a cask of rum that had been brought up from the hold and ripped open. Among them was the boatswain, who seemed to have taken charge. They were all dipping their tin cups into the cask and drinking, a large part of the rum trickling down their beards and over their clothing. So far, there was no fighting. I turned to Toine.

"Don't they seem calmer?"

"Don't count on it, my boy," he answered. "We'll probably see some pretty strange things soon if the rum doesn't kill them first."

Feeling very weak, I went back and stretched out on the hammock. Hunger gripped me, and thirst, too, but

I did not dare say anything to Toine who was suffering as much as I and never complained. Besides, what could he do about it? There was hardly any water left, and as for the flour meal, we were probably wise to avoid eating too much of it. Suddenly I had a mental image of the man I had killed. When I sank into a semi-comatose state, he appeared before me with a red flower on his forehead that grew and grew until it became enormous. The petals opened at an increasing tempo and then, from the center, a stem sprouted suddenly. Like a pointed finger, it came toward me slowly, ready to suck me into the man's cranium. I began to scream, and I must have screamed out loud because I felt myself being shaken.

"Hey there, cabin boy, shut up."

Toine was bending over me. Although he tried to make his voice gruff, I saw a compassionate look in his eyes.

The dawn was as black as muddy compost. The stars had fled and the night seemed to last forever. A silence as heavy as the heat hung in the air. The crew must have been wallowing in rum. Toine, who had returned to his hammock, no longer spoke, but in the shadows I could see his eyes gleam like those of a cat. The impalpable presence of suspense was all around us.

Suddenly we could hear stamping as if a thousand little paws were running on the deck. Toine leaped from his hammock, shrieking words I could not understand. He ran to the porthole; then, having looked, returned, saying with a broad grin the likes of which I had never seen on his face before:

"Can't you hear, lad? That's life that's falling from up high. Rain! At last we can drink all we want!"

He went to the door, unlocked it quickly and went out. Following immediately, I found him stretched out on the deck, his mouth opened wide, avidly lapping up the providential tears. I stretched out beside him and drank and drank until I was breathless. At the same time I rolled around voluptuously in this heavenly liquid, and in the end finally fell prey to a veritable delirium. Toine put an end to it by tapping me on the shoulder.

"Come on, lad, that'll do, now. Come, we'll give the men a hand."

Reluctantly, I got up and followed him. A few yards away the crew, greatly reduced now in numbers, were busy unfurling the big sails. They did this without hoisting them and consequently had endless trouble holding them steady facing the sky; the rain pouring down made the sails so heavy that the sailors had all they could do to hold them up.

Toine and I added our efforts to theirs. I must confess that it was not without some repugnance that I helped them. The frightful scenes we had witnessed were too fresh in my mind. Toine, however, spoke to the sailors in a way that could be described as almost friendly. For a moment this astonished me. But I learned later at great cost that men are as vulnerable to suffering as they are to joy.

Chapter 4

THE RAIN had stopped. The galleon's sails were finally hoisted and the casks that we placed here and there on the deck were full of that precious gift that the heavens had so graciously dispensed. Calm reigned once again in an atmosphere of interrupted dawn where inky black ran into dark gray. A ray of sunshine occasionally managed to emerge from a gap in the sky and illuminate an extremely calm sea that resembled an immense lake of tar.

Far, very far away, the muffled sound of thunder could be heard. As it moved rapidly closer, lightning began to streak the leaden sky, while the sea quivered and rippled under the impact of a fresh wind that had just arisen. In no time at all the sea began to sway up and down as if it were beginning a dance. One by one the sails puffed out on the mast, ridding themselves of the rainwater. Once again they became as white as angels' wings. The ship gradually moved low in the water, then began to quicken its pace as the wind blew in the rigging like a song of departure.

In unison, we all shouted our joy. After a moment, Toine put his hand on my arm.

"That's not the end of it. Now we have to steer. Come, let's take a look at the navigation cabin."

The boatswain was already there, several maps spread out in front of him. At our approach he glanced up, a look of complete bewilderment on his face.

"Hah! I see," Toine said in a voice pungent with irony. "The captain had the last word."

"And with you as well," the boatswain answered churlishly. Then more softly: "You've sailed the seas with him for a long time. D'ye know where he hid the instruments?"

"First you have to figure out what our last position was," Toine replied.

"Yes, but how?" answered the boatswain. "All I can find are maps that haven't been used. I'm sure the others must be with the instruments. I've searched everywhere in this damned cabin but haven't found a thing. And to sail without navigating equipment," he continued, but now he was shouting, "is like sailing blind."

"We've got the stars," Toine said calmly.

"Oh, sure, sure," the man answered, staring at Toine with a nasty look in his eyes. "And can you tell me who the hell knows how to read the stars on this damned boat?"

"Sure, I can tell you," Toine replied even more calmly.

At this point I thought that the boatswain was about to fall flat at our feet, the victim of a heart attack. His face turned a purplish red and the eyes that stared at Toine almost popped out of their sockets. Toine, his hands in his pockets, chewing his everlasting quid, looked at him, his head to one side, an amused gleam in his lively eyes. He seemed to take a mischievous pleasure in the other's growing exasperation which he did nothing to appease, rather the contrary.

"Well, who?" yelled the boatswain.

Toine shifted his quid to the other side of his mouth, ejected a long stream of spittle and, with perfect nonchalance, let fall: "Me!"

Then I saw him suddenly change completely. He pulled himself up to his full height and in a harsh voice said:

"Without me you can't do a thing. Just get that into your head, you and your rotten pals. I'm perfectly willing to navigate for you, but on one condition: I'm to be made captain right away. If not, to hell with you! As for me, I haven't much to lose anymore."

At first there was silence. Then the boatswain, his jaws taut, his fists clenched, stepped close to the cook, as if to touch him.

"Tell me, Toine," he hissed between his teeth, "do you take me for a damned idiot? You, the captain? You must be crazy!"

And as he spoke he pointed his right index finger at

his temple and turned it around and around. Toine looked at him contemptuously.

"Maybe I am, but you can take it or leave it. Go tell the others, and get a move on because we're going around in circles. If you like, you can also tell them I'm not against you're being second-in-command."

The boatswain opened his mouth, thought better of it, and turning suddenly, left without a word.

"And there we are," Toine said when he was certain that the boatswain was out of earshot. "It's settled. And now I'll tell you something, lad. I'll be lucky if I can tell the difference between the Great Bear and the Southern Cross."

"Well, then," I asked in a panic, "what's to become of us?"

"That's what I'm wondering," said Toine, shrugging his shoulders and chewing his quid. "But, to begin with, someone has to take charge of those brutes. Later, we'll figure out a way to collect all their weapons. After that, well, it'll be God's will."

This was the first time I heard him mention God. And though I can't think why, it sounded an unpleasant note. Was it perhaps because I had deserted God along with my childhood? But I had no time to wonder about this. The boatswain had come back.

"It's okay, chief," he said defiantly, "you've been made captain. But they don't want me to be the only second-in-command. They want two of us."

"In that case," said Toine, wrinkling his small eyes, "tell them that for the time being they're sailing before the wind, and tell them too, if I'm captain I don't take orders."

The boatswain seemed stupefied by the answer. But he went off once again without uttering a word.

Meanwhile the wind was blowing with increasing force and the ship was listing dangerously. But nobody seemed to be paying the slightest attention to this. Through the large windows of the navigation cabin we could see the sails all filled out.

"If they lose their stiffness, even a little, they'll tear," Toine said.

He stuck his head through the opening of the door and shouted into a megaphone that I had not seen him take:

"Lower the mainsail!"

I sensed hesitation over there, at the other end of the deck. But it was short-lived. Someone repeated the order and at that moment Toine found himself promoted to ship's captain without even knowing how to navigate. In different circumstances this would have been funny.

The day passed without untoward incident. Although extremely weak from lack of food, we all took courage. Night fell. Toine pointed out a star to follow, one he had doubtless chosen more or less at random, then took me to his new quarters, the captain's cabin. A large room with plenty of fresh air, it contained two bunks. By some unfathomable miracle it had not been plundered.

"We'll be better off here," Toine observed.

He began to search everywhere but discovered only an instrument of sorts which he examined with great care before showing it to me.

"You see," he finally said, "with this thing, when it works, which unfortunately isn't the case now, you can determine the latitude."

"Really? How does it work?"

"By measuring the height of the sun above the horizon. It's called a sextant. But, in any case, nothing's lost because we've no maps to indicate our position."

I let Toine choose his bunk and then settled down in mine. After so many nights spent in a crude hammock, to which no prior experience had inured me, this unhoped-for comfort would have delighted me had it not been for the painful cramps in my empty stomach. Very soon, however, I fell into a deep sleep.

Chapter 5

WHEN I AWOKE I found myself alone in the cabin. The ship was tossing; its frame and hull creaked terribly. I sat up in my bunk and glanced toward the porthole. Enormous waves, white with foam, swelled and broke, then sank to the depths. The spectacle impressed me deeply, but I decided nonetheless to go up on deck and join Toine, who was probably in the navigation cabin.

I climbed up but had a hard time opening the door to the companionway. Just as I thought I had succeeded, the impact of an incredibly powerful wave sent me scurrying downward. I tried again and this time I managed, in the interval between two waves, to hoist myself up to the deck. Bending low, I ran as fast as I could in the direction of the cabin and dived into it just in time; behind me a wave broke with a roar.

Toine was not there. I looked through the large windows and saw him, holding the wheel. He was certainly taking his role as captain seriously! Not a soul was in sight. Toine was a remarkable spectacle, standing alone in the midst of the gale, struggling with the helm against the unleashed elements. The mizzenmasts and foremasts without their sails, which had been lowered, looked skeletal. But the sail of the bowsprit at the stem of the ship, which the men had not been able to lower completely, alternated between pointing toward heaven and dipping into the sea like a flag of death.

Surging waves washed incessantly over the deck. Frantic, I began to wonder how I would be able to get to Toine. I simply could not remain in the cabin a minute longer; alone, I was far too uneasy. Finally, I decided to try at whatever cost. Ten times, I narrowly missed going over the side. Toine, I realized, was all the while shouting something to me that I could not hear. Finally, one wave, more powerful than the others, literally catapulted me into him. Continuing to grip the helm with one hand, he seized and held me with the other until I finally recovered my balance.

"Go over there," he said, designating with his chin the base of the helm where a rope to which he was attached had been tied.

At the same time he again gripped the wheel with both hands and righted the ship, which had been listing dangerously.

"You came just in time to give me a hand, lad," he added. "It takes at least two to hold on to this damned wheel."

"And where are we heading like this?"

"That, cabin boy, nobody knows. To avoid any argument about the direction we should take I gave orders to head straight out at the dawn."

The wind was shrieking frightfully. Ever wilder grew the dance of the ocean. The galleon rose and fell endlessly and the mainmast swayed to and fro like a drunkard. But freed of its weight, the mast held firm. The bowsprit, on the other hand, encumbered as it was by the sail, could not withstand the strain. A moment later the sail was unfurled so suddenly that it snapped.

Together the two of us had a hard time hanging on to the wheel. It swung uncontrollably from port side to starboard.

More than an hour after I had joined Toine the boatswain appeared. The astonishing ease with which he came toward us attested to his long experience with storms. He shouted to Toine:

"It's my turn to take the watch, captain."

I tossed an admiring glance at the cook who, with such apparent ease, had managed to impose his authority. But once back in our cabin Toine told me he had to knock down a sailor who had tried to stab him that very morning. The man had refused to obey Toine's order to lower the sails. After this incident, however, the others were inclined to obey without arguing.

Our clothes were soaked. We had to change into dry ones. This I did with some difficulty. The ship was pitching so violently that I rolled to the floor as I was pulling on my trousers.

"Lad," said Toine, laughing heartily, "you'll never make a good sailor. Come on," he continued, his voice now gruff, "sit on the floor to dress, if you can't manage standing up."

At that very moment we were staggered by a wave that broke over the deck with a terrible roar. Another soon followed. Above us we heard a crack, accompanied by the sound of crashing wood, breaking and giving way.

"Good God, it's that damned deckhouse that's gotten the hell away from us! We'll be going backward soon," Toine shouted. "We simply have to change direction."

Seizing a rope from under the lower bunk, he firmly tied one end around his waist. He threw me the other and explained quickly as he opened the cabin door: "You're to come with me on deck, but not right away. Stay on top of the ladder and hold me until I get to the helm. Then, I'll pull you."

We rushed toward the ladder. Combining our efforts, we pushed back the door to the companionway, then Toine climbed up to the deck. Despite the roar of the storm I could hear him bellowing furiously.

"What's the matter?" I shouted, sticking my head out of the hatchway.

"Those imbeciles are a bunch of freshwater sailors. They don't even know how to keep a sail secured. Take a look at the foremast!"

And sure enough, the thing was bending like a young weeping willow. The wind, with unimaginable force, was lashing its sail, every inch of canvas spread wide.

Toine leaned down and stuck his face close to mine.

"Now listen carefully, lad. You've already gotten me

out of one mess. Here's a chance to do it again. I've got to go and cut that mast; with that bitch of a sail all we do is go around and around and the water's washing over the sides. If I don't put a stop to it, I won't give us an hour before we sink. So, go to the cabin and bring the ax. It's under the bunk."

I ran down and was back in a minute.

"That's fine, lad," Toine said. "Now, hold on!"

And he slid into the foam of a wave that swept him off like a leaf.

I could feel him at the end of my rope like a fish at the end of a line. Suddenly the boat veered to one side and I caught the full lash of a wave. I tumbled down the ladder, but unwilling to let go of the rope, I had no way of breaking the fall. The shock was jarring. Had it jarred Toine even more? I clambered back up. There he was, pulled back to the starting point. At the sight of me he grumbled:

"One more spill like that and we're done for!"

He got up painfully. "Come on, we'll start over again."

I wondered where this little, dried-up, temperamental, middle-aged man got his inexhaustible energy. He was extraordinary. What a will of iron he must have to overcome the extreme weakness that plagued both of us!

This time he managed to reach the mast. He had already cut the ropes and was about to start on the mast when two members of the crew, shouting and gesticulating, rushed toward him. They probably wanted to prevent him from going on with what he was doing. But at that moment the boatswain, doubtless realizing that the mast had to be cut, arrived upon the scene and intervened. Whereupon the two sailors flung themselves at him. I was perhaps the only one to notice the enormous wave about to break over us. I drew my head down between my shoulders and held on to the rope with all my strength, leaning as much as possible against the ladder. It seemed as though the entire ocean was surging over me. When at last I could raise my head I saw Toine hugging the mast while the three others were rolling all the way to the rail. Another wave from the ship's stern dragged them the length of the deck. They gave no further sign of life. A fresh sea lifted them for a moment and then they vanished forever in the folds of the tempest.

Meanwhile Toine had gone back to work. Suddenly I heard a crack, followed by a muffled noise. I glanced quickly in his direction. The old devil had managed to cut down the foremast. But there was no trace of him. Panicked, I began to tug at the rope. But with every fresh wash of the waves I had to give way and I feared that I would eventually discover a drowned man at the end of rope. He finally came into view, his head bleeding. The sea had become less violent and the ship seemed to be forging ahead again. I managed with some difficulty to drag Toine to the cabin and hoist him onto the bunk. He could scarcely breathe, but he was alive. The gash in his forehead did not seem too serious. Fetching some rum, I raised his head and got him to swallow a few mouthfuls. Several hours passed before he opened his eyes. In the meantime, the sea had redoubled its violence. We were now in the very center of the storm, which reigned supreme over the ship, tossing and rolling it as if it were a toy. Twice I climbed up to the deck but saw no one. The wheel, left to itself, spun in the void at a rapid clip. Not knowing how to control it, I had no intention of trying. In such a sea I might have broken my arm. Finally I returned to the cabin and sat beside Toine.

He was still unconscious. His eyes were open but they had a vacant look, and he did not recognize me. I placed compresses on his forehead and forced him to take small swallows of rum, but all this was of no avail; he remained inert. Helpless, I watched the day fade, a prey to melancholy thoughts. My hunger was becoming intolerable. After a while I could think only of one thing: food. I was prepared to devour absolutely anything! I could not recall seeing Toine throw away the remains of our rotting flour meal, but neither did I remember seeing it in our cabin. Thinking it unusable, he had probably left it in the galley. At this moment the rotting flour meal seemed a sublime delicacy. Hesitating no longer, I started for the galley.

The end of the day had brought no lessening of the storm and, when I stuck my head outside the tarpaulin spread over the ladder, enormous waves beat against me. I quickly withdrew and waited awhile before trying again. Nothing on earth could have induced me to give up. The fourth try proved successful. I was careful to close the door, otherwise everything below would have been inundated. Hanging on to whatever was within reach, I continued to make my way toward the galley. It took an incredible amount of time to get there. I feared I would be washed overboard at any moment, but finally managed to get inside. What a disappointment was in store! All the cupboards were battered in. Even the futtock plates holding them to the floor had been torn loose. Traces of a struggle and bloodshed were almost everywhere. The surviving crew members, once they discovered Toine's reserves, must have battled over them. I drank a little from our store of rainwater and this momentarily relieved my hunger. Then I began my search anew in the hope that some other hiding place might have eluded the marauders. Unfortunately, I found nothing save a few traces of flour in the bottom of a sack which, naturally, was empty. In despair, I decided to return to my cabin. Suddenly, a pistol shot punctuated the noise of the howling tempest. Through the porthole I saw the last survivors of the crew locked in combat for the only remaining lifeboat. This was their final struggle for life and they fought furiously. However, a wave of extraordinary force suddenly washed over them, carrying off everything — men and lifeboat. At the same moment, the mainmast shattered on the deck with a frightful din. At once the galleon, gathering speed, began to spin. Although I know nothing about such things, I was convinced that we were caught in a whirlpool. Moving between two gigantic liquid walls, I began to make my way toward the cabin. The sea seemed to have opened up as if to swallow us. At last I lifted the hatchway and slid down the ladder.

I found Toine seated on his bunk. Thank heaven, he had regained consciousness! In a few words I told him what had transpired and described the whirlpool in which we seemed to be trapped.

This last bit of news appeared to shake him. Rubbing his tired face, he said:

"We're caught in the heart of the cyclone. Like the *Flying Dutchman*. Are you sure we're the only ones left on board?"

"Yes, I'm sure."

"Well, then, lad, so much for that. The two of us will have to get the boat out of this, if it isn't too late."

He stood up as he spoke and grasped the end of the bunk to steady himself. He'll never make it to the deck, I thought to myself.

I misjudged him. Not only did he reach the deck but both of us, after a good deal of difficulty, I must admit, got to the helm in one piece.

A veritable wall, liquid and circular, surrounded us. And we were spinning giddily within it. Millions of circles formed by this liquid mass refracted the ghastly color of the twilight sky. Toine grasped the wheel only to let go.

"Too late," he said. "A hundred men together couldn't resist such pressure."

As if drawn by a magnet, the galleon was nearing the center of the whirlpool. It was spinning faster and faster. We had to lie on our backs. Owing to the ever increasing rate of rotation, the centrifugal force became so strong that it pinioned us to the deck. And since the deck was almost vertical, we had the appalling sensation of standing at attention to witness our own agony. The sky above us seemed scarcely wider than a pair of hands. We were sinking into the abyss. Suddenly there was a tremendous noise like an explosion, then a kind of extraordinary sigh. The pressure that had held us fast to the deck diminished and the ship began to rotate more slowly. At the same time it righted itself, although continuing to list dangerously. The downed mainmast rolled incessantly from side to side, smashing everything as it moved. Now the ship was lying low in the still-heaving sea. Toine shouted:

"We've got to get down the other side. It's going to turn over. If we stay here we won't have a chance."

We clung to the ropes, using them to slide the length of the hull to the sea. Although I did not know how to swim, I gave it scarcely a thought. Besides, I felt that this was happening not to me but to someone else. Had it not been for Toine I would probably have drowned. He held my head above water, then finally managed to catch hold of the mainmast, which had been floating a good distance from us. In a kind of fog I glimpsed the ship one last time, its keel sticking out of the water. Then I lost consciousness.

Chapter 6

I OPENED MY EYES and at first did not realize where I was. Then the deafening noise of the sea and the wind, which seemed to be pushing all hell before it, brought memories back in a rush in all their ghastly reality.

The darkness about me was total as I lay stretched out on the mast. The cords that lashed me to it precluded movement of any kind. Toine? Where was he? Hopelessly I began to call him. There was no response save the noise of the wind that drowned out my voice. Feeling more and more acutely that I had been forsaken, I wept softly.

The cold, together with my extreme weakness, sent violent chills up and down my body, causing it to quiver like the strings of a violin. Night was dragging on. I thought it would never end when, all of a sudden, a ray of the moon pierced the inky black sky. Although it seemed like a light brandished by death, this pale shaft comforted me. I felt calmer. After a while it began to rain. I opened my mouth wide to slake my thirst. Then the rain ceased, the wind subsided and thunder began to rumble ominously, soon followed by the appearance of an extraordinary galaxy of stars. At that instant I felt that I was passing into another world, another life. The feeling did not last long but I knew that until my dying day I would never forget this strange sense of a sudden transition.

The darkness that had once again invaded the sky suddenly dissolved and the firmament returned, full of new stars, larger and more brilliant than any I had seen before. Wild, feverish thoughts came to mind: God, tired of the monotony, had redesigned the heavens. Again I lost consciousness.

I was completely astonished to find myself still living and lashed to the mast. The dawn was nearing its end, the sea almost calm. I raised my head as high as the cords permitted and spotted Toine, recumbent like myself, at the other end of the mast. He seemed unconscious. I called to him weakly. He did not answer. I longed to draw closer to him, but how? The seawater had swollen my ropes and it was impossible to untie the knots. Now that the dangers of the tempest were receding, I saw myself caught in another trap from which there seemed no escape. Moreover, I was suffering atrociously from cramps and from a violent pain that had taken hold of my spine. For hours the rounded wood of the big mast had been pressing against my ribs and chest. Now it finally bore down on me and I could only breathe in gasps.

All around us was the liquid void. The day grew lighter and lighter and on the horizon a curious red hue preluded the sun — a color akin to blood. Slowly it spread. I had never seen anything quite like it and for a moment I imagined I was having hallucinations. I was amazed to see that when the sun finally rose it was entirely speckled with this same strange color, as if it had suffered a wound. I could scarcely believe my eyes. An exclamation made me start. Turning my head, I saw that Toine, who had finally regained consciousness, was also staring at this extraordinary phenomenon. I called to him weakly. Breaking into a smile, he said:

"Have I gone mad, lad, or do you see what I see?"

"I see the same thing you do," I answered. Then, impelled by a morbid thought, I added: "Doesn't it look as if it's bleeding?"

"Oh, shut up!" Toine cut me off brusquely.

Meanwhile, the red mottled disk continued to rise. It dispensed a light the color of baked brick. The heat had increased considerably. After a struggle, I was finally able to loosen the cords and went to sit beside Toine, dipping my feet in the water. We did not speak, torn between contentment in being still alive and the superstitious fear inspired by this untoward occurrence, so contrary to the usual order of things — this sun that was already as hot as a forge fire. Soon the heat became unbearable and, at ever shorter intervals, we were obliged to dip into the sea to cool off. Because of our weakened condition, this exercise soon exhausted us. All around we could not help perceiving the same hopeless void.

Toward the middle of the day the appearance of horrifying animals plunged us into terror. Truly monstrous, at least ten yards in diameter, they resembled giant Medusas or octopuses, their tentacles as thick as tree trunks, with the exception of one peculiarity that made them even more repulsive: umbrella-shells strangely speckled with red. Their numbers increased at an alarming rate and they swam between the waves looking, because of their numbers, like an immense bloodstained sheet endlessly strung out.

When these monsters appeared we stretched out on the mast, carefully avoiding any contact with the water. We replaced the cords, attaching them to our feet, our waist and under our arms in order to remain immobilized on the mast. And now we watched with anguish as the sun began to set, thinking of the terrible night in store for us in this abominable place.

As the day declined, the sea, losing its transparency, took on a rusty hue. And of the monsters we saw none, save the few that surfaced occasionally. They appeared even more iridescent in the crimson light which the gathering dusk drew around us.

"It must be the reflection of the devilish sun!" Toine remarked.

But when the blood-red orb drowned in the infinite expanse of the sea, the animals continued to glow a phosphorescent red in this night of unfamiliar stars.

Toine made a brave attempt to speak of the noctiluca and protozoans that at times abound in the sea. "When the sea is rough they look phosphorescent," he remarked. But this did not explain the color of blood that had uninterruptedly enveloped us since daybreak. At last, he said: "Lad, I've never seen such a thing and I really believe we're in another world."

Fear permeated us so completely that despite profound exhaustion we dared not yield to sleep. The sea had turned to oil, the sky had strange depths, and a terrifying silence hung over us. Our mast remained totally immobile. A malevolence impossible to define emanated from our surroundings. I, for my part, had the sensation of being swallowed up by a grotto of boundless dimensions, its vaults studded with enormous shining worms as vitreous in life as in their own light.

The aquatic monsters continued to pierce the sea's surface without making the slightest sound.

"Have we become deaf?" I asked Toine.

"No, lad," he answered, equally perplexed. "We're not deaf because we hear each other when we talk."

Asking no more questions, I surrendered to the torpor that gradually possessed me.

"Look, lad, it's starting all over again!"

Toine had crawled closer and was gently shaking my shoulder. I opened my eyes to see his ravaged face. Only his eyes preserved their extraordinary brilliance.

At that moment I resented his rousing me from a sleep that had banished all thought and delivered me from the torture of thirst, which again was painfully constricting my throat and guts. This drove everything else from my mind so that I was quite indifferent to the repetition of the phenomenon. Weakness caused thousands of little gold specks to glitter before my eyes. The sight of all the water around us only aggravated my thirst. Realizing my condition, Toine said:

"Listen, lad. Moisten your mouth with seawater. Give it a try. But watch out. Don't swallow any."

I followed his advice instantly. But having moistened my lips, I could not resist drinking a mouthful. I anticipated a terrible burning sensation, but to my stupefaction and joy the water proved as soft and fresh as any that came from the clearest of springs. I quickly dipped my face in it. There was no longer the slightest trace of yesterday's monsters.

Toine looked at me sadly. Of course he thought I had gone mad. But after watching me cup the water to my lips repeatedly, he succumbed and did likewise. His astonishment equalled mine. When we had quenched our thirst I asked: "How is this possible?"

He shrugged. "Oh, this at least can be explained. Sometimes it happens that a big river empties into the sea and pushes its waters far, far ahead of it. But what about all the other queer things? No, lad, let me tell you, I've sailed all the seas in my bitch of a life and believe me, I've never seen nor heard anything like it!"

During the day we managed, though not without

difficulty, to capture an octopus. It was of normal size, about a yard in diameter. Several times we had to follow it deep under water. To cut open its sac was no mean affair and, when we finally succeeded, we were splattered by its blackish ink. When, at last, it lay still, we divided its rubbery, viscous flesh. In our famished stomachs this filthy meal was without equal, and it enabled us to recover some of our strength, to say nothing of our badly impaired spirits.

The heat, as unbearable as before, was beginning to produce mirages. Mountains appeared before us, then beaches; boats headed in our direction. The first mirage did not disappear as rapidly as others; on the contrary, it persisted disquietingly. What we saw was an awesome chain of mountains, volcanic in origin, red and rising toward the sky like the Tower of Babel. At every moment we expected it to disappear. But at the end of the day it was still there. Hope began to take root in our hearts. Then our joy burst forth. Land! We were going to set foot on land! We threw ourselves into each other's arms, weeping like children.

A gentle current edged us toward these mountains. As we approached, they looked more and more like an enormous rocky wall. The effect was overpoweringly oppressive.

"If only we find something to eat there," Toine said. "We haven't even seen a single bird around here."

"Never mind, we can always fish," I answered, thinking only of the solid earth that soon would welcome us.

"Yes," Toine said with a touch of reticence.

Evening came, surprising us when we were just a few miles from the coast. For me, the night promised to be euphoric. Not for a long time had I felt so light-hearted. But this did not seem true of Toine. Several times I heard him murmur: "A world upside down; yes, it's a world upside down." I even had the impression, before falling asleep, that for the first time the old sea wolf was praying.

Part Two

Chapter 7

ONCE AGAIN a scarlet light preceded the sun. This was
the moment our mast chose to run us aground along a
coast of small coves. The little bay, curving into soft
rocks, was edged by a tiny beach of rust-colored sand. I
was the first to set foot on it. How can I describe the joy
I felt in finding myself once again on solid ground? I
skipped, I sang, I laughed. Toine, for his part, did not
seem to share my enthusiasm. In fact, he seemed un-
mistakably downcast.

"Aren't you happy?" I asked him. "This time I really
believe we're saved."

"Sure, lad, of course I'm happy," he answered in a
falsely hearty voice. Realizing that he was trying to con-
ceal his true thoughts, I did not persist, reluctant at
that moment to spoil my own pleasure.

All around us the rocks were of the same red color
that prevailed everywhere in these strange parts. The
sand under our feet was extraordinarily fine, like light
dust. I picked up a handful. It was, one might say, im-

palpable, and slipped through my fingers. The little I was able to retain I got rid of by tossing it into the sea. The spot where it fell immediately turned blood red. Taken aback by this, I turned to Toine. He, too, had seen what had happened. The expression of his face chilled me. For a long time we stood in silence near the spot, which was disappearing. Then Toine turned away, shrugging.

"We'd better get busy and look around these parts before night falls."

"The main thing is to find something to eat," I replied.

It took us a good hour to climb the rocks that encircled us because, although not high, they were extremely soft and crumbly. For every yard we advanced we had to go back three a second later — all this in the midst of a reddish powder that was blinding and suffocating.

Once we reached the top we saw the awesome chain of mountains that had given us such a distressing sense of oppression the day before. It was some twenty miles distant. Nonetheless we could distinguish dark spots — probably woods — spread out at the mountain's foot, as if they were fertilized by its shadow. To reach it we would have to traverse a red, arid desert.

"First we've got to find some way to carry water with us," Toine said.

"But how can we?" I cried. "We haven't a thing but our hands and our ragged clothes!"

"That's just it. We'll have to find something. If we

don't find a way to protect ourselves from the heat, we're done for."

We came down toward the coast, this time choosing a different beach. Here, unlike the little bay on which we had landed, everything was vast. A gigantic ring of red sand, as fine as talcum powder, encircled the base of a thick red wall that towered toward the sky. Majestically, it displayed time's erosions — wounds shaped like grimacing masks resembling giants solidified or petrified by countless centuries. There was no vegetation. The atmosphere was sepulchral, but there was no odor of mildew, as if nothing were left of the compost heap made by the dead.

We began to skirt this natural wall. It was split in several places like the one we had descended to go to the beach. We did not speak, impressed as we were by so much hideous beauty.

When we reached the other end we found nothing that could be used to transport water. And now hunger again made painful inroads. Toine swore incessantly between clenched teeth. This was his way of venting his suffering. We had to get past the cliff that protruded into the sea and impeded our progress. To retrace our steps was out of the question since we knew we would find nothing there. Still grumbling, Toine went into the water first. I followed but lost my footing almost immediately. He pulled me up by the hair, saying gently:

"Excuse me, lad, I forgot that you can't swim. Hang on to the cliff and stay close to me. There's no danger."

I did not share his opinion. The cliff was crumbly and each jagged edge that I grasped crumbled between my fingers, the dust falling into the sea. As had happened a few hours earlier, when the sand came in contact with the water, the sea instantly turned red wherever the dust touched it. We ended up swimming not in clear water but in blood.

"What a filthy mess!" Toine said, grabbing me at the very moment I had let go for the second time. From then on I kept gulping mouthfuls of water. What I feared most, I believe, was not drowning but swallowing this disgusting water that nauseated me.

The rocky spur was finally skirted. Discovering another beach similar to the one we had just left, Toine said with controlled rage:

"This is getting monotonous!"

"But look! I see something over there," I cried, pointing to large black areas along the red wall.

He peered for a moment in the direction I had pointed to, then affirmed:

"Those are grottoes. Maybe at last we'll find something different. Let's go."

As we came closer, the grottoes increased startlingly in size. They soon began to resemble enormous jaws ready to engulf the mother cliff in their black void. It took no less than two hours to reach the first grotto. Its proportions were fantastic. Compared to it, we seemed no larger than the light grains of sand underfoot. From the top of the vault which half crowned its entrance, its walls grew bigger until they were a hundred yards wide. Its depth, incalculable from the spot where we were standing, seemed to lose itself in the night.

I must confess that my mind was not at all at ease when I entered this colossal cavern with Toine at my side. In fact, I was on the verge of fleeing. My companion must have been aware of this, for he said, grasping my arm firmly:

"Come on, lad, don't lose your nerve."

His voice was instantly carried off and, like a string of prayers recited aloud during Holy Week, it echoed for several long minutes throughout the immense vault glutted with darkness.

Our eyes, still filled with the intense light that reigned outside, adjusted with difficulty to the sudden shadows, and we moved forward blindly. Beneath our feet the sand had given way to earth hard as concrete and cold and damp as a tombstone moistened by winter rain. Our gestures and even our breathing, seized by the echo, mingled with the shadows in a fantastic rhythm. Enraged, Toine began to swear emphatically. The cavern vibrated; then suddenly there came, far off in the distance, a frightful sound of falling stones. An explosion followed. Then silence. But it was not total silence. A strange whistling could be heard, like the noise of rapid breathing, accompanied by a sound that resembled the muffled beat of a heart. It was terrifying; we remained frozen to the spot, not even venturing to speak. Finally the noise diminished until it ceased altogether. At the same time our eyes, now accustomed to the darkness, could make out the fantastic walls of these extraordinary subterranean passages. If only we had never had to look at such a sight! It would have spared us the nightmare vision that shortly presented itself.

Here and there statues gradually emerged from the shadows. There were many, each in a different pose. Their features were frightful, tortured, filled with anguish, as if the sculptor had wanted to shape them all into a unique kind of suffering, his great artist's hands tolerating only the hideous death brought about by fear. Their bodies were chilling. Men and women, each with a distinctive form, vulgar or elegant, were thrown into relief, as if they had all been cut from the same stone. We could discern mothers holding children in their arms, and their faces, bending close to the little ones, retained in their stone grimaces an imperceptible maternal smile. Among all these statues representing the human form were others — figures of animals and birds among which the albatross, with large wings fully spread, was the most numerous. Curious primitive utensils were strewn about this hallucinatory museum; a few bones, also. Here and there black spots marked the location of hearths. In great haste we picked out some terra-cotta receptacles in the form of crudely made amphorae. Without casting a parting glance at this workshop of a master as talented as God — but without His gift of grace, of life and laughter — we retraced our steps.

Much to our relief we found ourselves once again in

the brilliant light of the open. For a moment it blinded us.

"What a strange place!" Toine sighed after a long while. Since our weird discovery we had not exchanged a single word. Holding at arm's length one of the amphorae he was carrying, he continued:

"Look, lad. Whoever was able to make the perfect statues we've just seen can't even mold an object as simple as this properly. Don't you think that odd?"

"Yes!" I cried. "I hadn't even thought of that!"

"Anyway," Toine went on, nodding his head, "the important thing is that we won't suffer from thirst. We've got something to store enough water in until we reach fertile land. Once we get there, we'll find something to eat."

Far from sharing his optimism, I wondered anxiously how I would be able to hold out until then without eating anything at all.

We returned to the beach for our water supply, then climbed up the red wall again, crossing as we did so one of its passes. Not very wide to begin with, the path grew progressively narrower so that by the time we reached the top we were advancing sideways, like crabs. During our climb, the same indefinable muffled beating that had so upset us in the grotto began again, the sound coming as before from a great distance.

We were now crossing the desert of fine sand that a light breeze blew about in small, circling cascades. Far off, the dark area at the foot of the gigantic mountains, mingling with the deep red of the sky, looked increasingly unreal as the day waned. We entertained the absurd hope of reaching the mountains before nightfall. Meanwhile, I suffered so greatly from hunger that I began to feel giddy. Several times Toine had to hold on to me to keep me from falling. Although he was experiencing the same torture as I, he kept showering me with words of encouragement. Our progress slackened considerably because of our condition. The sun, in its twilight decline, was already setting the horizon aglow, making it look like a heated steel blade. The sky, gradually invaded by the night, took on a violet hue. Not for one instant since daybreak had it permitted a single bit of blue to show through. Finally the black curtain of darkness fell and the unfamiliar stars resumed their appointed places.

"Let's stop here," Toine said. "If we keep on we might go around in circles and it'll just take us longer to get there."

We stretched out on the sand. It was as soft as velvet. The breeze, continuing to blow gently, wafted a few grains over our faces, barely brushing them, feeling like a small child's caress.

We did not speak. But in the shadows I assumed that Toine, like myself, was examining the sky where nothing usual or familiar appeared. Was this the place I had heard one of my teachers talking about when I was a child? If I remember rightly, he called it Olympia. The ancient Greeks believed it to be the abode of the gods. For a moment I was tempted to speak to Toine about this, but I told myself that my mind was wandering and rejected the idea. Closing my eyes, I had but one thought and it pervaded my entire being: to sleep.

Little by little sleep overcame me. But it did not rid me of the muted fear that had been my faithful, intimate companion these last few days. I felt my heart beating strangely. Toine's voice made me jump.

"Lad, don't you hear anything?"

"No," I answered lazily, on the verge of dozing off. "I just feel as if my heart were beating too hard."

Toine's voice went on, but I heard it as if in a dream:

"You're wrong, lad, it's not your heart you're hearing. It's the same noise we heard in the grotto of the ravine. I think it's coming from inside the earth. Put your ear close to the ground."

But nothing could tear me from the profound numbness that enveloped me.

Chapter 8

I WOKE UP suffering from terrible stomach cramps. The day had scarcely dawned and the sun was still hidden behind the tall, mysterious mountains which were gradually becoming tinged with red. Toine moved beside me.

"Well, lad, did you sleep well?"

"Yes, but I'm hungry!" I answered, pressing my hands to my aching stomach.

Toine made a gesture of helplessness.

"Oh, better try not to think about it for the time being." He sat down and took hold of an amphora and handed it to me.

"Here, drink a little water. It'll help."

I drank a few mouthfuls without much conviction. Almost instantly my cramps seemed less painful. Toine had turned his old, wrinkled face toward the mountains.

"Lad," he said in a voice that was almost solemn, "I didn't close my eyes last night. I've had plenty of time to think. Well, what I'm wondering is whether we're still on our own planet, on earth. You see, a place like this, with that light, those stars, different from any others — really, I've never heard of anything like it in all my bitch of a life." He stared at me with his little black eyes. "Tell me, what do you make of it?"

I gestured in such a way as to indicate my ignorance. He shrugged.

"Of course, how could you know? This is your first trip. You don't know anything about the world. Come on, boy," he added, standing up, "it's time to get going again."

The dark area at the foot of the mountains began to stand out more clearly. Although still very far away, we were now convinced by its green color that it was a forest. As we moved closer, the forest became plainer. The sun was ablaze, making our unceasing struggle against exhaustion even harder. To cap it all, when we stopped to rest a little and to drink a few swallows of water, we had an unpleasant surprise. The precious liquid had lost its limpid transparency and had turned bright red. We had no choice. We had to drink it. It was tepid, and this was enough to intensify the feeling that we were drinking blood.

We resumed our march toward hope. With the approach of evening we finally perceived the first signs of vegetable life: the ground was more solid, the dust rarer. A thin, sparse grass sprouted. So great was our hunger that we flung ourselves upon it, devouring it right on the ground without even taking time to pull it up. Were we imagining it, or did this grass truly have nutritive powers? In any case our hunger pains definitely subsided. That night we even slept better.

Early the following morning, after drinking a little of our putrid water, we left. A few hours later we reached the forest's edge at last.

Immense trees held their heads high, mingling the green of their foliage with the purple of the sky. Their enormous trunks were laden with creepers curiously shaped into ringlets the thickness of an arm. Toine walked up to a tree trunk and tried to pull a ringlet off. Unsuccessful, he gestured to me to come and help him. Our combined efforts proved vain. Only the thin bark of the creeper yielded. Stripped as it was, it slipped through our fingers, leaving them saturated with a red, sticky sap.

"We need something that can cut," Toine said, searching the ground. He spotted a flat stone, probably a relic of some volcanic eruption, and thought it sharp enough to cut the enormous woody stem. I wondered why he wanted so badly to cut it. I could hardly believe that he meant to eat it; but, sensing that this was not the right moment, I asked no questions and watched him press the stone against one of the ringlets with a to-and-fro movement. Suddenly he uttered an exclamation and tossed the stone far from him.

"Good God! It's moving!"

At first I, too, thought I had been having hallucinations. Now I could cast aside all doubt: very slowly, like a gigantic boa constrictor, the creeper contracted, coil by coil. It undulated like a living animal. At the same time a strange noise, a kind of gasping sound, seemed to escape from the trunk it was constricting while sap the color of rubies ran from minuscule and innumerable wooden fissures. Toine turned and looked at me, dazed.

"Have I gone crazy?"

My own expression told him that I had seen the same thing.

"Come, lad," he said, taking my arm. "Let's get out of here, this place is cursed!"

"But where can we go?" I asked despairingly.

"There's still the mountain. Maybe it'll be different on the other side. But first we must find something to eat!"

However, the farther we penetrated into this imposing forest the more remote seemed the possibility of finding anything to eat other than the grass we had torn from the ground. In our state of extreme weakness this semblance of food, while it calmed our hunger pangs, could scarcely give us the necessary strength to go on. For several hours we walked beneath this grandiose and impressive vegetal overhang. Every now and then I fell to the ground, refusing to go on any farther. Had it not been for Toine's friendly but energetic insistence, I would surely have given myself up to death, struggling no longer to preserve so miserable a life.

The day almost ended when we arrived within sight of a clearing containing numerous huts in a more or less dilapidated condition. Because of the silence that reigned, it never occurred to us that life might exist here. We entered the first hut. In it we found a few of those strange statues we had already seen in the grotto. On the ground lay a large bag of unidentifiable material, half corroded by time; from it issued a few green shoots. Toine bounded over to it, shouting, "Potatoes!"

He was right: these were young potatoes just beginning to sprout. We devoured them joyfully.

Sated as we had not been for a very long time, we began to explore the tiny village. It did not take long. Each hut contained the same statues of people or of animals of every kind. Only the poses differed. The expressions were all invariably tormented with the exception, however, of the children, whose features remained relatively normal. In all these mysterious museums, various objects lay on the ground, objects made of wood, stone or bone, crudely fashioned. Neither Toine nor I knew enough about art to make any comparisons, yet we were both extremely puzzled by the incredible disparity between utensils and figures. Moreover, in each hut, the hearth site was filled with burnt ashes and the ground was littered with wooden bowls containing desiccated food, as if a sudden misfortune had forever frozen the inhabitants of the village to that spot. And yet there was no trace anywhere of combat nor any sign of volcanic lava. Toine kept repeating:

"It's not possible! You'd think they were vitrified and that they realized what was happening."

I finally asked him exactly what he meant by that and he explained:

"Do you remember the stone I picked up this morning to cut the creeper? Well, it had been vitrified. Probably by the heat of a volcano in eruption."

"Well, then," I said, "that's probably exactly what happened here."

"No. It looks that way but it's impossible. You can be sure that if an avalanche of lava had fallen over the area, no vegetation would have grown here again. But even that," he went on, "would have been possible only if the wind was able to carry the pollen and seed far enough."

I did not understand a single word about vegetable life reproducing itself beyond the oceans. Nor did Toine attempt to elaborate. He merely placed his hand on my shoulder, and a smile that was most comically reflected in each of his wrinkles lit up his face. As the horizon began to glow, he picked up two strange-looking stones and rubbed them vigorously together. A rain of sparks burst forth. Still rubbing the stones, Toine walked over to the sack that had contained the potatoes and, after a few moments of patient waiting, succeeded in setting it on fire. We ran to the various village huts searching for anything we could find to feed the fire. Soon the flames were dancing a ballet. In the hut's total darkness, the light cast by these twisting flames made the statues around us seem even more weird. In the shadows they appeared to be moving.

We stretched out on the ground near the fire. Once again, among the crackling embers, we caught the sound of a muffled, rhythmic beating that seemed to arise from the center of the earth.

We took turns getting up to feed the fire. We wanted it more for the light it shed than for warmth. Finally I sank into a heavy slumber.

Chapter 9

I AWOKE to broad daylight. The sun was slipping along
the somewhat battered branches of the hut, streaking
the ground with luminous rays. Toine had gone out.
Alone, I began to daydream. I had awakened with a
sense of well-being the likes of which I had not known
for a very long time. Was it because of the potatoes I
had eaten the day before? Had they helped me to recover some measure of energy? Unfortunately, in looking about, my eyes fell upon the statues, and all my
anguish, more acute than ever, returned. A strange
premonition took hold of me and immediately I thought
of Toine. Good God! I said to myself, I hope nothing
has happened to him! I got up quickly and went out.

In the brilliant red light the silent village was an extraordinary spectacle. I looked for Toine. Not seeing
him anywhere, I entered and inspected all the huts but
he was not in any of them. I decided he must have
gone into the forest. Losing no time, I rushed toward it,
hoping also to appease a hunger that again was plagu-

ing me. As I walked, I saw many trees laden with the coveted fruit; unfortunately, the branches were much too high and I could not reach them. In the end, I decided to fall back on the shoots of the creepers. I had just pulled one up from the earth and was preparing to eat its tenderest part when, to my horror, it moved in my hand. It coiled itself up like a snake, but its movements were infinitely slower. Instead of getting rid of it, I stared at it in bewilderment. When it coiled itself around my wrist, I quickly recovered my senses and tried in utter disgust to throw it away. But it seemed to be stuck to my skin. To rid myself of it I literally had to tear it off. Imagine my stupefaction to see beads of blood on my wrist where the creeper had squeezed it! Examining my wrist more minutely, I also detected very faint traces of suction. Overcome by my discovery, I tried to resist the thought that this vegetable world, however outrageous, was also carnivorous. On the ground the creeper continued its reptilian movements.

Absolutely terrified, I went off under the vast green canopy in search of Toine. Through the sparse gaps of the unkempt foliage the sky looked down like so many red eyes. The hot breeze that rustled the leaves gave me the unpleasant feeling that these glances from on high were mocking me. To add to the disquieting effect of the strange forest, there was not the slightest sign of animal or bird, not even of those insects that usually make a blade of grass into a lively little world, not unlike our own. I called Toine's name from time to time but it was all in vain. My anxiety increasing with every step, I finally arrived at the river. The water was soft and fresh. I took a long drink, then, not knowing which direction to follow, I decided to walk along the river bank. The crystalline sound of a waterfall attracted me and I obeyed an impulse to find it. In my solitude, the presence of this natural sound of flowing waters was familiar and, to my surprise, I suddenly began to feel a warm affection for it, as for a brother.

The cascade was farther away than I had first thought, but when at last I found it I had no regrets, although there was nothing to indicate that Toine had come this way. The view before my eyes was spectacular. From the center of a rock, gigantic and as smooth as a wall, tumultuous waters poured forth and fell in a sumptuous shower of white foam that fanned out and sparkled in the light like a river of diamonds. The river was thus made to leap more than a hundred yards. The banks, fed by the fresh water, were adorned with giant, bright-hued flowers. The smallest flower was easily twice my size. The grass was plentiful, a beautiful green. I approached one of the flowers, a species I did not recognize. It was white, curiously edged with lavender and its corolla was yellow. As I neared it, it slowly closed. Suddenly I was positive that it was advancing toward me. Panicked, I drew back quickly. I was just in time. Opening again swiftly, it stretched forward and then, like a fish net, collapsed on the ground on the very spot where I had been standing only a few seconds before. There was a terrible sound of suction, then the flower closed again and very slowly resumed its initial position. Nothing but bare earth was left of the spot which, for an instant, had been covered by its petals. Under my horrified gaze it had sucked up every-thing — grass and shrubs — just as it would have sucked me up had I not retreated in time. Cold sweat ran down my spine as I watched the enormous trans-parent stem begin to digest its prey. Overcome by ter-ror, I stood there as if hypnotized. Finally I managed to tear myself away from the horrible spectacle and run off. The extraordinary beauty of the place, which at first had filled me with wonder, now made me tremble with disgust. I say disgust because fear no longer had a place in my feelings. I was beginning to understand why the souls that sojourn in Hades remain there with-out apparent revulsion. Is not disgust the beginning of acceptance? If acceptance is inevitable among normal beings, surely it is logical for those who remain deaf to the very questions that might save them.

I shall probably never know how I managed to go back through the woods. All I remember is that, at a given moment, I found myself in the village of the stone inhabitants. At the same time I heard myself being called, but still dazed by my emotions, I did not think to respond. A sound thump on my back finally brought me back to my senses. Toine stood beside me, his arms filled with strangely shaped fruit. He offered me some; I seized them and ate avidly. They had hardly any flavor but I didn't care, so intent was I on satisfying my hunger. Once I had eaten, I recounted my adventure to

Toine. He listened, nodding his head. When I asked him whether he believed my story, he must have guessed my thoughts, for he said:

"Calm down, lad, I saw strange things this morning too. We've really come to a place that's cursed. We've got to get out of here, no matter how. We won't do it if you lose your head the way you did a few minutes ago."

While we were talking we walked back to the hut that had sheltered us during the night. We sat down on the ground and remained silent for a moment while our grimacing hosts watched over us in the shadows. As we began to eat the fruit again I noticed that the piece I was munching had a red flesh, but it was a normal shade of red, like blood oranges. It had a very pleasant taste and was as big as a watermelon. I asked Toine by what miracle he had managed to collect the fruit. He answered:

"All I had to do was bend down and pick them from the highest branches."

Seeing my stupefied look, he continued:

"No, lad, I haven't gone crazy yet, though I don't know why. Listen, I'll tell you what happened. I went off early in the morning. The red day was just about to begin and the stars seemed to be watching over it. You were sleeping so soundly I didn't want to wake you. It didn't take me long to reach the middle of the forest. But — and this is what's peculiar — once I got there, I still saw stars that the leaves usually hide. I'll tell you why. All around and in front of me giant tree trunks lay on the ground, as if, during the night, woodsmen had cut them down. I was hungry and at first all I could see was the fruit lying there, within reach. It was like a miracle! I ate enough to bloat my belly. Can you imagine that? All I had to do was stoop and pick them up.

"After that I gathered a supply to take back to the village. But once I didn't have to think of filling my stomach, you know something? I began to get more and more worried. There must have been a reason why all those giant trees were lying on the ground like that, their tops facing the great chain of mountains I could see in the distance.

"At first I was almost reassured when that blood-colored sun began to come up over the mountain wall that blocks out the horizon. But not for long. Can you imagine? Suddenly there was a horrible crackling of unseasoned wood multiplied a thousand times, and the entire forest began to stand up. Yes, lad! Don't think I've gone crazy and that I'm talking nonsense. Not a single tree trunk was on the ground. They were all getting up. Do you want to know how it seemed to me? Well, from the largest tree to the smallest shrub, the forest looked as if it was bowing to the mountain chain! I thought I was dreaming, believe me. The entire forest praying, all the trees bending down, then standing up again as if they'd been kneeling! I swear, if the ground had started to speak to me I couldn't have been more dumbfounded."

I looked at Toine, wondering, despite his warning, whether he had taken leave of his senses. He guessed what I was thinking from the expression on my face.

"So you think I'm crazy? Believe me, I'm no crazier than you are."

We lapsed into silence. I could see, however, that Toine still wanted to talk. After some hesitation he asked:

"Did you hear anything last night?"

"No, I was sleeping too soundly. I don't even remember dreaming."

"Well, then, maybe I'm mistaken. Listen to the end of my story. While the forest was kneeling I heard, from the far-off mountains, something that sounded like a song. It seemed a little like the noise the wind makes in the halyards. Then, from the ground, came the same rhythmic beating we've heard so often. But this time it was much louder and the ground under my feet vibrated terribly, as if its guts were moving."

He suddenly stopped talking, his dark eyes fixed on the grimacing shadows of the statues. What had just occurred to him?

After a while he went on: "Lad, I finally began to wonder — after all, it's not impossible in a place like this — if it isn't the heart of all the statues we've seen, beating under the earth. I can't believe any more that it's the work of a mad artist. Nor the work of God, who's supposed to be good. So I see only one possibility: we're at the gates of hell. Maybe it's the fire of lost souls that's reddening the sky. But this nature that's become corroded can't understand what grieves men's souls. Neither God nor the Devil would enjoy playing such a comedy."

I really did not understand what Toine was trying to say, but of one thing I was sure: if we did not find a way to get out of this place quickly a terrible disaster would befall us.

"What shall we do now?" I asked.

Apparently deep in thought, Toine started and looked at me for a moment as if he had never seen me, then he answered:

"First of all we must go back to the river. We're going to need water. After that, we'll take the road to the mountains. I'm sure the key to the mystery lies there."

The thought of returning to the hostile place I had left in a state of terror only a short while ago made me tremble. I said nothing, however, and helped Toine search the hut for receptacles other than our amphorae, which were too small to be useful.

"Come, give me a hand, lad, I think I've found what we want."

Toine was pulling a dark bulky object. As I drew near, it looked like a big terra-cotta demijohn. It was stuck between several of the stone figures, so we had to move them first. Taking a thousand precautions owing, I must confess, to a certain superstitious awe, we began to displace the statues. Suddenly, one of them lost its balance and toppled before we had time to right it. It broke with a dull thud and the head, which had come off, rolled a few yards like a ball.

We stared with amazement at the remains that littered the ground.

"That's impossible!" Toine exclaimed. "Why, there's even a skeleton formed on the inside!"

It was true. There, before our eyes, a complete skeleton was spread out, the only difference being that it was made not of bones but of petrified earth like the exterior of the statues.

Without saying a word, Toine turned away and began anew to disengage the demijohn. As for me, I could not take my eyes from that frame of stone ribs or the spinal column, now broken in the middle, that somehow looked so frighteningly natural. Its appearance of life was nothing but similitude, but so true, so analagous, that one would have liked to fondle these remains as one rocks a child.

"Leave it," Toine finally said. "I feel like you; they're our brothers but, like misfortune, they make me afraid. Let's go and get the water. Come on. And let's enjoy life because I think we haven't much more time."

He loaded the demijohn onto his back and we left without a backward glance.

Outside, a light wind had begun to blow, making music with the green leaves of the vegetable world. They were waving, swaying, curling, encircling the trembling, fissured tree trunks that oozed red tears like the tears that run down the cheeks of grieving children. I could not help thinking that here a world of life was marching toward death.

Toine, who was walking a few yards ahead of me, suddenly stopped, put the demijohn on the ground and bent low, shouting:

"Come quickly, lad! You'll see, I'm sure these are delicious!"

When I saw what was happening, I flung myself at him, screaming:

"No, don't touch it!"

But he was already struggling with a creeper at least three times bigger than the one I had such difficulty eluding a few hours earlier. Too upset by what I had seen at the waterfall, I had not mentioned this adventure to Toine, so he was not on his guard.

Despite the speed with which I went to his help, the horrible woody stem succeeded in enveloping not his wrist, as in my case, but his throat. And now, little by little, its coils were squeezing it. Although I pulled with all my strength it did not give way. Despairing, I watched as Toine's face turned an ugly gray. He was suffocating. His eyes protruded from their sockets. Not knowing what else to do I started to bite the creeper furiously, gradually cutting it with my teeth. Then, what I no longer dared to hope for finally happened: the living cord relaxed suddenly. I just had time to jump aside to avoid being snatched in turn. I let it continue its coiled dance on the ground farther away and kneeled at Toine's side. Stretched out on the earth, he did not move. He had not, however, lost consciousness and he looked at me with haggard eyes. When he recovered his breath he said:

"Thanks, lad, you saved me from a painful death."
Rubbing his throat where big blue blotches were beginning to appear on the swarthy skin, he continued:

"I must take off my hat to you. You've sure got courage! Weren't you scared?"

I told him about my own experience.

"Oh, now I see why you acted the way you did. You'd been through the same thing! So you were able to save me."

"Yes and no," I answered. "If I had thought to tell you about it you'd have been more careful."

I picked up the demijohn and loaded it onto my back; then we resumed our walk over this cursed land.

We walked side by side. From time to time Toine rubbed his throat but did not complain. In his wrinkled face, his smile had died, replaced by astonishment, not fear. Noticing that I watched him furtively, he said:

"I'm really sorry, lad, that you've got to be alone with me in my waking nightmare. But you'd better realize that if we lose our heads we'll be working against ourselves. Here, everything is a mystery. Don't expect to find a solution. Death is on the prowl alongside of life — here as everywhere else, only a little more so, that's all."

He said this to quiet me. But as he talked I felt rise within me a desolate, final solitude. Toine, I could see plainly, was following, without fear, the path of acceptance. Yet I wondered if the astonishment I read on his face was not that of someone who realizes he is still alive. My companion's old heart was worn out, and I was convinced that it continued to beat only for the sake of his young friend.

We no longer spoke, but continued to move forward

beneath the green canopy of this mysterious world. I knew that Toine would never again be the same. The natural song of the cascade reached us at last, and I saw a gleam of interest light up his dark eyes. I began to hope that perhaps everything was not lost.

On the green slope of the tender turf we lay flat on our bellies to drink the clear water. After quenching our thirst, we remained stretched out, relishing in silence this feeling of well-being that we knew, alas, was illusory, so great was our desire not to believe for a moment in the tenacious anguish that gripped us like a leper.

The shadows had once again taken possession of the motionless sky. Night had not yet descended but the stars were about to appear. It was a moment of waiting — the only moment in this monstrous mystery that resembled moments in normal places. The silence was broken only by the distant song of the crystalline waterfall which the immense carnivorous flowers watched over jealously. Finally the black night inundated this cold communion of two humans who still had hope, and the nameless stars, one by one, clung to the large secret vault. I started as Toine spoke in the darkness:

"We should have brought something to make a fire with. In a place like this we can never find dry wood. Everything is a deadly dull green."

Chapter 10

As OFTEN HAPPENED, I went to sleep without realizing it. I seemed to hear Toine stamping his foot beside me and grinding his teeth with impatience, probably because I did not wake up fast enough to suit him. Half furious, I finally raised myself on my elbow and grumbled:

"All right, all right, I'm getting up."

But my bad temper disappeared when I saw Toine, or rather his shadow, leaning over me to whisper:

"Keep quiet, lad, and look!"

His tone of voice, the kind used only for good things that are nonetheless awesome, impressed me more than a kick in the shins. Besides, it was not exactly Toine's habit to swoon with admiration before any old thing. So I got up, whispering in turn:

"What is it?"

Staring straight ahead of me I saw nothing but the forest in the silvery tones of the pale dawn. I turned toward Toine.

"Well, what of it? It's only the day that's dawning."

"In the middle of the night? Have you ever seen the day dawn at night, lad? In a place like this where there's never a moon? Besides, you know very well that here the day is red."

It was true. How could I forget it? But then, what else was going to happen? I felt my blood congeal when the noise I had mistaken for Toine's angry foot stamping when I slept, again made itself heard. I leaned against the arm of my companion.

"Can you hear?" I asked in a low voice.

"Yes, lad," he answered in a strangely calm tone, "it sounds like the beat of a giant's heart under our feet."

Now the grinding noises began again, accompanied by the kind of cracklings that the trees of our forests produce when they are two-thirds severed from their trunks by woodcutters and begin to bend toward the earth. At the same time it grew lighter and lighter, a cold, luminous, thick light, similar to mercury when it flows into water. The entire forest was visible. Slightly arched, the tree trunks emitted groans like breaking wood. I recalled Toine's story. Was the same phenomenon occurring again? Soon I could no longer doubt it: the enormous forest was beginning its incredible greeting. It was bowing toward the mystery. Like nuns taking the veil, it touched its green forehead to the ground. The groans exacerbated my nerves, already so severely tried. The tree trunks were now at such an angle that at any moment I expected to see them break completely off. Already the leaves of the long branches were touching the soil of the underwood. Then the branches spread out like arms crossed, and the high verdant crests arched over the ground, displaying the soft colors of their budding shoots. My eyes were caught by the highest of the distant mountains beyond us. It was as red as a forge fire. And the pounding, which for a moment had lessened, suddenly resounded again with a devilish violence. There was a long sigh, then the pale light gradually darkened and the forest resumed its place, quietly rearranging its leaves in the black sky. Silence reigned once more. Only the mountain, appearing to lean against the darkness, continued for a brief moment to glow before fading very slowly at last, as if in a dream. The unfamiliar stars began to sparkle brilliantly.

"It's over!" Toine said simply.

He stretched out again on the ground. I lay down at his side as he continued:

"Now we can sleep. It won't move any more. I stayed awake on purpose to see if what I saw last night would happen again."

It was then that I asked the question that burned my lips.

"How did you have the courage to pick the fruit?"

"First of all, when I went into the forest, the trunks were already on the ground. I was so terribly hungry, I only saw the fruit and I asked myself no questions. Besides, the light that made you think it was daytime wasn't there. I'll admit that if it had been I wouldn't have touched those trees for anything in the world.

Didn't you have the feeling that we were watching through a shroud around our dead bodies?"

Exhaustion adding to our emotions, we were no longer in control of our reactions. We sank into a sleep that was very much like a faint.

When we again resumed contact with reality (but was it truly reality?) the red light of day was upon us. We both remained stretched on the ground, listening to the liquid sound of the nearby cascade which accompanied a light whisper of wind that slipped between the leaves of the resuscitated forest. Suddenly Toine broke the silence.

"Lad, how about taking a bath?"

I looked at him with some surprise. He said with a smile that made his wrinkles dance:

"Why not, after all? It'll be good for us."

He stood up and began to take off his clothes. Then he dived into the river. A moment later I saw his head bob up in the middle of a current.

"Come on in, you can touch bottom here."

But no sooner had he finished talking than he disappeared suddenly. He was not long, however, in surfacing. Then he began to swim toward the bank. When he emerged from the water he stretched out full-length on the grass without saying a word. Intrigued, I moved closer to him. His thin, sinewy body, unbelievably youthful for his age, was shaken by chills.

"What on earth happened for you to be in such a state?" I asked.

A few minutes passed before he answered. Then, turning toward me with a strange look in his eyes, he said in a muffled voice:

"Lad, I'm already beginning to doubt what I've just seen. At the very instant I called you to join me, the gravel under my feet suddenly gave way and I felt something, as if I were being sucked down. At first I thought I was on quicksand and dived underwater to see how I could get out of it. And then I realized that part of my leg was caught, not by quicksand but by a hole shaped like a mouth, and it was moving! Lad, I had to pull apart two real lips of sand to get away!"

As he finished he smiled sadly.

"Of course you think I'm crazy."

"Of course not," I answered in what I hoped was a reassuring tone. After everything we had already experienced it never occurred to me to doubt anything my companion said. Despite the horror rising within me, I looked very deliberately into his eyes and continued:

"Whatever happened in the river doesn't matter. Haven't you told me over and over that if we're going to get out of here we mustn't let ourselves get discouraged? So let's keep our minds on one thing: finding the solution."

As I spoke I could see my old friend's face relax and a little amused gleam appeared in the depths of his dark eyes. When I had finished he emitted a long whistle between his teeth, then cried admiringly:

"Well, upon my word! We've suddenly become a man! A real one! Now there's no reason on earth why we can't get out of this mess, on old Toine's word of honor."

Coming from him, the words gave me real pleasure. He was right. Now I felt I was capable of handling anything, even the worst possible situation. Of course, my anguish had not vanished, but I was finally growing accustomed to it. Courage, I think, is no more than that.

Chapter 11

WE FOLLOWED the riverbank to the waterfall. It was already very hot. The fresh morning air had taken wing like a final breath. Before long we arrived at the cascade with the giant flowers. Seeing them again caused a chill to run up and down my spine. It even seemed as if new flowers had blossomed since my last visit. But was this possible in so short a time? Toine, who looked at them with interest, murmured, as if to himself:

"There's something odd about these flesh-eating plants here."

I did not know what he meant. As for me, I must confess that I had no desire to seek answers to anything. The mere sight of those vegetal monsters frightened me too much. To avoid looking at them I let my eyes wander over the spray blown from the cascade as it shone in the red light.

The sound of Toine's voice made me jump.

"Lad," he said, "instead of daydreaming, help me figure out how these plants that feed only on flesh can manage to live in a place with nothing but minerals or vegetables."

Toine's remark surprised me at first. Indeed, how could this upside-down world exist at all since there was no apparent life anywhere, neither in the sea and river nor on earth or in the air? Save for the stone statues resembling humans and animals, there was no indication whatsoever that a carnal life had ever existed in this place. And yet our very presence was proof that a human being could live normally here.

"Look, lad, you'd say this is a world made only of silence," Toine said, thus seeming to answer my thoughts.

"No, not entirely," I answered. "The cascade makes as much noise as any cascade, last night the trees moaned rather noisily, and finally there's that beating that seems to come from inside the earth and never stops."

"That's true, but I don't think those noises belong to the world as we know it. Why, even the fruits are unfamiliar. Maybe you're going to say that's natural, that they change according to the region. But I can tell you that I've been to every part of the world and I've never seen anything like this. The same is true of the trees. I'm perfectly willing to admit that there are some different species, but here they're all different and that just isn't possible. It's too much for my old brain! I'm too old to trade reality for dreams. Besides, I don't want to scare you, but isn't it true that this morning

I barely missed being swallowed up by the river's bed?"

I shivered at the thought. We filled our demijohn with fresh water from the falls, then headed for the forest, resuming our walk toward the mountain.

At first we had an easy time. The trees were fairly sparse, the underbrush was no impediment, and we advanced almost noiselessly over the moss-covered ground, circumventing the living creepers that hung from the high, motionless but vigilant branches. Alas, just as we were congratulating ourselves on our uneventful progress, we suddenly realized that the trees were becoming far more numerous and that from the low-hanging creepers thorny shrubs had sprung up, reproducing in miniature a second forest. As if that were not enough, the day began to decline.

Long before the sky, which we glimpsed through occasional gaps in the foliage, had grown dark, we found ourselves caught by the darkness beneath our green roof. Extremely reluctant to spend the night in this forest, we continued to go forward in the hope of discovering some kind of clearing. At every moment we were obliged to tear away the creepers. Like serpents, they coiled their fibrous bodies around us. The heavy demijohn which we took turns carrying impeded us considerably. Yet we could not leave it behind.

Toine was the first to stop.

"Lad, we can't go on like this anymore. We aren't even sure that we're walking in the right direction. We'll have to spend the night here. Oh, I know that everything here's unfriendly, but what else can we do? There's no light to guide us."

We stretched out side by side in a small clearing devoid of creepers. But how could we go to sleep when our anxiety was so acute? Far above us, in the leaves of the top branches, a light wind blew, making a sound similar to the tread of a tiger or cat, while from the bottom of the earth the muffled beat mounted, and on the ground the crawling of the creepers made a reptilian sound.

We did not say a word. What was the use of voicing our fears? We knew we were both thinking of the same things. After a long time I began to hope, in spite of myself, that the night might pass without mishap. I was on the verge of sleep, ready to sink into it.

Suddenly I sat up, my nails pressing into Toine's arm.

"Do you hear that?" I screamed, completely terrified.

The infernal noise with which we were all too familiar could again be heard. The entire forest vibrated in one long shudder, accompanied by the heartrending creaking of tree trunks beginning their bowing movement. But this time it was infinitely more terrifying because we were at the very center of a phenomenon that could conceivably crush us. Toine also began to scream and our cries mingled strangely with those of the tree trunks. We rose, bracing ourselves for the massive weight that seemed about to descend upon us.

"Let's slip over to the foot of the nearest tree trunk

to avoid getting crushed," Toine said, recovering his senses.

I followed his advice although I was astonished that a man like Toine could nourish the hope of escaping from the vegetal monsters around us. I found myself at the foot of a tree, but without Toine. In my terror I had unwittingly walked away from him. I called him, but in this medley of groans, cries and creaking not even a bugle could have been heard. I finally gave up and clung to my tree much as a shipwrecked sailor clings to flotsam. I could feel the pulsating life of the tree. Its sap began to drip over me. Tears of blood, I thought in horror. When I heard the rustling leaves brushing the earth I decided it was all over. Like a child I closed my eyes in a futile gesture of self-protection.

An enormous sound, compounded of cracking and of leaves moving over the ground, was followed by silence. From the depths of the earth the hammering recommenced, and very soon the noise became deafening. Finally it ended and then I heard Toine calling me. My eyes still closed as if awaiting death, I could not bring myself to answer. It's useless, I told myself, only a miracle can save us. When his voice grew more insistent I finally opened my eyes. The forest had returned to normal and was bathed in an indefinable light. In this beyond-the-grave phosphorescence I could see that the tree trunks were righting themselves. I also saw Toine, who was equally luminous, a few yards away. Suddenly I stood up.

"Over here, Toine, I'm here."

He turned his head toward me and then approached, a look of astonishment on his face.

"Do you know that you're shining like the forest?" he said when he reached me.

"So are you."

Toine's face fell.

"In that case, lad, it's because there's a curse on us, like the forest."

So great was my joy to find myself still alive that my only reaction was to burst out laughing. This infuriated Toine. But he calmed down quickly and put his hand on my arm.

"Excuse me, lad, I must be losing my mind over all these strange happenings."

I merely smiled. Seeing him shine in this curious fashion, I finally began to think that perhaps he was right after all to believe we were cursed. At last the disquieting light diminished and the night was once again calm and serene.

Precisely as before, we both sank into a slumber that was like a faint. Something other than anguish or fatigue — so it seemed to me — made us drop into a torpor akin perhaps to catalepsy. When we came out of it, big red rays were breaking through the green roof of the forest. My companion — I had noticed this before — emerged from this lethargy considerably more aged and bitter. It suddenly occurred to me that perhaps there was something about this nightmare that he was concealing from me. I wanted so much to believe that once we crossed the mountains we would find salvation!

"Are you hungry, lad?" Toine asked, rising painfully.

"Of course I'm hungry," I answered with a certain impatience. "But what difference does that make since there's absolutely nothing to eat."

"We'll see about that."

Toine disappeared behind a shrub and I saw him return almost immediately, his arms filled with fruit. I was amazed. What self-control he had to touch the tops of trees that bent to the ground!

"Doesn't anything frighten you?"

"Sure," he answered, letting the fruit fall at my feet. "Hunger."

He was already biting into the pulpy flesh of a kind of enormous stone-fruit. I soon followed his example.

For a while we ate in silence. Toine was satisfied long before I. His appetite was less demanding than mine, probably because of the difference in our ages. Comforted by the frugal meal, our thirst quenched by the fresh water in our demijohn, we set off again on a path tinged with green and purple.

We advanced slowly. The forest was becoming inextricable and the thorny bushes scratched us cruelly. The living creepers gave us no respite, often forcing us to alter our course. Although the vegetable world was increasing rapidly, no animal life was apparent, not even those insects one usually sees dancing in the light of the underbrush. As humans we were in some way trapped between the mineral and vegetable worlds.

In this unaccustomed place all life's charity existed

only for these two worlds, as if a carnal God had no knowledge of the region in between.

At last we arrived at the edge of a clearing. Was it really prudent to go any farther? The grass that grew here was abnormally green, and there were those marvelous flowers, tender or violent in color, amazing in their great size. Although they in no way resembled the flowers of the cascade, there was no reason to believe they, too, were not carnivorous.

"Lad," Toine said in a resolute voice, "we've got to go through it. We've no choice."

He was the first to cross the edge of the clearing. What then was our surprise to see the flowers fleeing at our approach, with all the lightness and elegance of does. Astonished by this sight, worthy of a madman's delusion, we stopped in our tracks. The flowers also stopped.

Toine sighed: "We're to be spared absolutely nothing!"

"Maybe it's a nightmare," he added after a few seconds of silence, "but you'll have to admit that it's very beautiful!"

Indeed, how could one remain insensitive to this vast stretch of ocean green, where immense flowers swayed, retaining all the elegance and charm of normal flowers? An extraordinary perfume followed in their wake. In the background, very far away, great mountains could be seen, their crests lost in the red of the sky.

We followed the flowers until we noticed that they were leading us to a swampy terrain. To avoid being bogged down in it we had to head for the fringe of the forest.

Unable to cut through the woods, we found that our way was much longer. But at least we could walk normally and did not have to cope incessantly with creepers and thorny shrubs. I watched with some apprehension the shadows of the night slowly descending upon us. The idea of sleeping in the immediate vicinity of these flowers no longer appealed to me. I mentioned this to Toine.

"Don't worry so much, lad," he answered. "Nothing can be worse than that forest bowing down. What harm can the flowers do us?"

"You're forgetting the ones at the cascade. Didn't they attack me?"

"That's true. But these run away when we come near. So perhaps we needn't fear them."

Before stopping, we waited for night to fall completely. Then we stretched out on the cool grass. A heavy silence brooded over us, interrupted from time to time by the light rustling of flowers in motion. As the immensity of the sky gradually filled with stars, Toine suddenly exclaimed:

"You can imagine that as a sailor I've a good memory for stars. Well, tonight, would you believe it, they're no longer in the same place. So who's shifting about, we or they?"

Seeing that I did not understand what he was trying to say, he patiently explained:

"Just listen. It's not so complicated. If you go

straight north you'll eventually see the sky filled with stars from north to south. And vice versa. But the stars will always be the same, no matter where you are. They'd merely be more or less distant from the horizon. But there's nothing like that in this sky, the sky we've seen every night since we got here. So, either the stars are shifting about or we are. In any case, this universe is unfamiliar. I've never before seen a single one of these stars. I'm beginning to be feel sure that we're under different skies."

Toine's reasoning was certainly quite logical. I rejected with horror, however, the notion that we might be elsewhere than on our good old earth. What would happen then to hope?

I felt someone shaking me but I had been sleeping so heavily that I was reluctant to open my eyes. I wanted to remain alone in a night of my own. I had not reckoned, however, with Toine's strong grip. He continued to shake me.

"Come on, wake up, young 'un."

I finally opened my eyes. The sky was as black as a deep pit.

"Why did you wake me?" I said wearily. "I was so sound asleep!"

"For God's sake, can't you see? Look at the clearing!"

I turned my head. The entire glade was illuminated by the shimmer of the virgin forest living its silvery hour. But what seemed even more extraordinary —

and I raised myself on my elbows to see it better —
was the fiendish dance of the flowers, their petals glis-
tening in this unreal light like the leaves of a water lily
submerged in water. Along the rim of the mountains
the horizon was as red as the embers of some gigantic
fire and the earth vibrated from blow after blow, like
the heart within a frenzied breast. My eyes were riv-
eted to this bewitching scene. I wondered how I could
tear myself from it when the shadows, gradually moving into place, finally obliterated every trace of the
drama.

I could not go back to sleep. Neither could Toine.
We spent the last hours before daybreak surveying
this ominous universe. But nothing moved.

The vast clearing emerged again in the first light of
dawn. The flowers had disappeared. Only a few petals
— light specks in the midst of an ocean of greenery —
remained to convince us that we had not been dreaming.

Before starting off again, we ate some grass to appease our hunger. I noticed for the first time that our
skin was becoming curiously rough, as if mud had
dried on it. I mentioned this to Toine, who answered
wearily:

"We'll take a bath at the next river and it'll disappear.
It's nothing but dirt."

We did not allude to it again.

Skirting the vast expanse of moving earth, we began
to feel that we were going around in circles, never moving ahead. Toward the middle of the afternoon, how-

ever, we arrived, at last, at the outermost limit of what we had come to think of as a boundless area. Below, on a lower level, was a gorge, a veritable chasm that we would have to cross if we were to reach the mountains that rose up, majestic, on the horizon.

"We can't possibly get across that," I said.

Toine shrugged. "I don't see any other way to reach our destination. Look how the gorge disappears, to the right and the left. It's really a boundary."

A feeling of revolt, almost of hatred, rose up in me.

"But, really, what an absurd idea! Why should we make such an effort to reach those forbidding mountains? After all, there's no reason to believe we'll find salvation when we get to the top. In fact we might die of hunger or thirst."

"I know," Toine answered with infinite calm. "But do you really think you can survive here, in the middle of these damned woods? With these man-eating flowers, and all the rest? No, this is nothing for human beings. On the other side of the mountains maybe we'll have a chance of getting back to the kind of life we're cut out for. So, my boy, whether we die here or there, it's better to fight back. I'm as tired of all this as you are. If you don't want to go on, I'll play the game alone. And if I make it, I'll come back and get you. No self-respecting man could stand the thought of deserting a friend."

Toine's words, expressing bitterness quite as much as unshakable resolution, suddenly dissipated my fury.

"If one of us goes, the other must follow," I said.

"But how can we actually get to the bottom of the chasm?"

"By going over there," said Toine, pointing.

My eyes were caught by his outstretched arm. The strange crust that Toine attributed to dirt had grown thicker, and his legs and back, which I now examined attentively, were also covered with it. Seized by a terrible premonition, I began frantically to scratch mine. But it stuck to my skin like cement to stone. In a frenzy, I asked: "Are you sure it's dirt? You're hiding something, I'm sure of it! Please, I beg you, tell me what's happening to us!"

He answered in the same weary voice. "Listen, lad, you're not in pain, are you? Well, then, forget about it. It could be the heat that's cooking us."

I knew that he was trying to reassure me, that he did not, in fact, believe a word he was saying. Nonetheless, I did not dare to mention it again but instead screwed up all my willpower in an effort to overcome this new anguish that slowly, inexorably, invaded my mind.

Toine was leading me to the place he had spotted as the most propitious for our descent into the chasm. We started down. It was my turn to carry the demijohn, which hindered me considerably from the very start. Realizing at one moment that my feet were about to slip, I had to let go of the thing in order to hold on. It began to roll and disappeared from view.

"Don't worry," Toine said, sensing my despair. "I'd be surprised if we don't find water below. In any case, better the demijohn than you."

Toine's voice gave me the curious feeling that nothing more mattered. Was it the hope of discovering life on the other side of the mountain slope, or . . . no, no, I did not want to think of that!

After a long, painful descent our feet touched a rock. It was enormous and projected rather far out in the void. Falling flat on our bellies, we crawled until we could peer down into the abyss. Several fires lit up the bottom and we could see its extraordinary depth.

"Do you have any idea what that might mean?" I asked. Toine kept his eyes fixed on the bluish gleam which, by its very shadows, lent life to the dead surfaces of the gorge.

"No," he finally replied, "no, I really don't know."

We continued our descent even though it became more and more arduous. Two rocky walls enclosed us. A cloud of thick, evil-smelling smoke floated overhead and it began to grow warm. The red light of the day was rapidly declining. Soon, all that remained to guide us was the glimmering of the blue flames. Through the crusts that covered large parts of our bodies, the sweat oozed, thick and yellowish like pus. At the same time, and this was astonishing, the fatigue that had overpowered us disappeared. Was this due to the fumes from these mysterious hearths? I had no idea. But one thing was certain: we touched bottom in an almost euphoric state of mind. Toine was smiling again, his face wreathed in wrinkles that the disquieting crusts held fast. The fires were much farther apart than we had imagined when we first saw them from above. With a slight hissing sound they issued from the earth through small craters. We had no difficulty skirting them.

Now we had to climb to the other side. By some strange mystery, our strength had multiplied tenfold; we started at once to scale the wall. Discovering additional footholds here, we were able to climb with relative ease. This was fortunate, for hardly had we climbed halfway when the dreaded banging began to resound violently, causing a frightful trembling of the chasm walls. At the same time, giant flames that almost touched us shot up, unleashing an unbearable heat. I was about to relax my hold when suddenly everything returned to normal. The silent night settled over us with no other light save that of the unfamiliar stars.

Unable to go forward or back, we remained there, suspended, until dawn. Exhaustion once again enveloped us and, had the wall not inclined slightly, we surely would have fallen and crashed to the bottom of the gorge. The wait seemed endless. Below, meanwhile, the first fire began to burn again. It was instantly followed by a second, then a third. A minute later the entire chasm was ablaze. We experienced once more that marvelous sensation of strength and well-being we had known the day before. But, when I was able to make out Toine's features, I observed with horror that the filthy crust had spread alarmingly. In the eyes of my companion I read that my face had suffered the same transformation. We resumed our ascent without exchanging a word.

As we climbed, fatigue once again held us as if in a vise. I watched Toine furtively. His face began to look more and more like a mask, and I, too, reacting to the strain of this difficult climb, felt my features stiffen. We hoisted ourselves out of the enormous cavity at the very moment the sun chose to glow, tinting with lavender the heavens where the night was expiring. The crests of the imposing mountain chain remained hidden by the brightening shadows. A short distance separated us from the top. A level, desertlike plain of sorts seemed, at first view, easily negotiable, but this proved an illusion: scarcely had we set foot on it than we sank to our knees. It cost us a great effort to move forward at all. And when, the night having fled, the blood-red sun returned to its appointed place, we discovered that we were surrounded on all sides by a red powder, a disturbing reminder of the dried and coagulated blood that we thought had spent itself. This should have seemed terrible and appalling, but instead we felt all at once profoundly detached from the horrible, the monstrous. Our exhaustion, too, disappeared, and we were able to resume our climb without delay once we had reached the foot of the highest mountain. But despite the curious tranquillity that settled so mysteriously within us as we moved upward, I could not, without a feeling of aversion, look at Toine's face, which was literally turning to mud.

Chapter 12

THE MOUNTAIN consisted of the kind of silt found on rocks at the ocean's bottom, rocks so porous they resemble sponges. But unlike a soft sponge, the mountain was as rough and abrasive as pumice stone.

We had scarcely gone a hundred yards when we saw to our amazement a large number of the now familiar statues in human and animal form. All of them were stuck to the mountain. Oddly enough, I felt an almost fraternal affection for these earthen figures, while for the statues of the grotto or village I had experienced nothing of the sort. The higher we climbed this monstrous vitrifed sponge, the greater were the number of mineral ghosts attached to the wall of the mountain by their backs. Their beaks, snouts and mouths were joined in the expression of a single emotion: the fellowship of fear.

Relentlessly all that day we continued our ascent, talking as little as possible because every word caused severe physical pain. Frequently we exchanged glances, our eyes mirroring our horror. Little by little, as the frightful crust grew thicker, we felt ourselves turning to mineral. At last, behind a distant horizon which consisted perhaps of nothing more than emptiness, the great red disk sank toward the earth.

In the twilight a mass of mineral beings surrounded us, shedding a soft purple light over the declining shadows. The pulsating beat recommenced. As night took full possession of the sky, the plain and the woods came to life beneath the pale shadows already so familiar to us. A murmur like a whispered prayer mounted toward us. We were stretched out like statues, our eyes fixed on the forest, our backs stuck to the stone. Fear engendered fear. Those who have never known this feeling know nothing of terror. When, like a death rattle, the muttering arose, I felt, I must confess, that I was fast becoming like those earthen things all around us. From my poor misshapen mouth I managed to express my thoughts out loud. I hoped that Toine would hear me, and he did. Surely he was experiencing an anguish like mine, but with an abominable grimace he managed to laugh at it. To the very last, this extraordinarily courageous man would seek to reassure his young companion.

We returned to our silent contemplation. The forest emerged clearly now. The tree trunks and leaves gave out a silvery light and from the center of the mountain the pounding grew more and more violent, the shadows encircling us more luminous. So supernatural seemed this vision that in my folly I hoped it was merely a nightmare, that soon I would awake to find myself in a normal world. Toine's hand on my arm dispelled all illusion.

"Loo-ook!" he said.

Gloved with mud, his hand pointed to the woods where all the trees shone in a metallic light. I jumped up from the mountain soil suddenly and this made a strange sound. Sensing some dampness beneath my mud-encased hand, I examined the spot where I had been lying. From the spongy rock a thick, dark liquid oozed. I was overcome.

But Toine continued to point to the forest. In the celestial vault the stars sparkled with a cold light. The entire mountain was illuminated. Blue flames rose from the gulf we had traversed.

Slowly, beyond the desert of red powder, beyond the gulf and opposite the clearing, the entire forest bowed. This adoration of nature enthralled us. Meanwhile, the mountain had begun to vibrate violently. Then, as happened each night after this phenomenon, the stars paled and went out, one by one. At our feet, mysterious nature ceased to be visible — the night had snatched it from our diseased eyes. And now, we too were surrounded by profound darkness. We no longer felt anything, no longer were anything. Once again, the shades of oblivion enveloped us like a lead carapace. Soon we were no more than a pair of benumbed souls.

It was with the feeling of having very slowly climbed up from the bottom of a pit that I resumed contact with a world still inhabited by darkness. Along the horizon, to be sure, pink shadows began gently to beget the red day. But for the moment, the heavens, still empty, enjoyed their solitude. Hidden behind the wall of night, the plain was as yet nothing but darkness, as mute as a hole dug to infinity. With mud-caked lips I called to Toine, but my voice scarcely carried. Had I merely imagined that I was calling him? Or had I become deaf? Withdrawing into the hopeless agony of suspense, I closed my eyes and began to recite the prayers of time's rosary.

A sound I immediately recognized told me that Toine was working himself loose from the stone. Then silence, uninterrupted, fell.

Little by little, as the sky was about to explode into red, vague shadows formed. Finally, for the first time, the summit of the gigantic mountain appeared before us, high in the rose-tinted sky.

Like a jagged thorn it soared in the heavenly void. Countless shapes of all kinds, clinging in clusters to the mountain's flanks, seemed to continue their ascent toward eternity.

I turned with difficulty toward Toine to ask him if we should continue our climb, but my question remained suspended on my earthen lips. He was horrible to see! His mask of mud had become solidified, but his features, so molded as not to resemble him, made his countenance appear as if it were being refashioned. The only flicker of life in his poor old face was the look in his eyes. Their expression left me in no doubt about my own appearance. This should have driven me out of my mind, yet a strange calm inhabited me. Was this the beginning of renunciation?

Toine was trying to talk to me. But his half-opened stiff mouth could utter only unintelligible sounds. It was only when I saw him painfully trying to rise that I finally realized he wanted to continue our ascent. Did he still believe that we would find salvation on the other side of the mountain? I, for one, no longer thought so. I submitted to his decision without really sharing it.

It was painful to move. We had the feeling of being enclosed in a heavy constricting suit of armor. Frequently, to aid us in our climb, we would catch hold of one or another of those petrified beings. Breaking loose from the mountain, they would slide down and down toward the plain without stopping. Although the sun's position indicated that we had been walking for several hours, the crest of the mountain seemed as far away as ever. Happily, save for a feeling of extreme heaviness, we no longer felt either fatigue, hunger or thirst. But we were growing shorter of breath because of the thin rarefied air. It oppressed us and, in order to breathe, we had to open wide our misshapen mouths in a grimace similar to that on the faces of all the stone statues.

The slope grew increasingly steep, almost perpendicular. But this did not bother us. We stuck to the rock as if our hands and feet had mysterious suction cups attached to them. Slowly we rose toward the summit, so charged with promise and hope. At the same time our metamorphosis into minerals became hourly more noticeable, more repulsive. Our hands, our fingers, thickened by layers of earth, remained wide open. It was impossible to close them. Our limbs, deprived of flexibility, gave us the appearance and weight of moving statues. Far away, beyond the desert and the forest, we could see the sea. In it the red sun, all aflame, seemed to be contemplating itself. A massive silence reigned. When, at last, we reached the top, we were thoroughly exhausted but content and filled with hope. For a long time we rested, stretched out on the ground. We must have looked like two heaps of mud. The great moment had come. While negotiating the various stages of our journey, we had headed toward an objective that for us could only mean salvation. Having achieved our goal, what would we really discover on the other side?

We were afraid to get up and find out whether life really existed on the other side of the slope. Still recumbent, we gazed at the immense stretch of stone that covered the entire surface of the summit. In contrast to the flanks of the mountain, the rock was as smooth as the flagstones of ancient dwellings caressed by countless feet. In the center, shaped like a slightly raised bowl, was an enormous crater — an immense pit of sorts with a rounded border whose orifice was somewhat elongated at the top. Toine stood up. He seemed to have recovered his strength. I was perplexed to see him look around as if he were searching for something. Then I, too, rose. When I realized that not a single statue was on the platform, that all of them had apparently stopped short of the summit, I understood. Unless they fled from it, I told myself in anguish. Fear gripped us again like an old friend as we started, at last, to cross the extraordinary esplanade. We moved forward like automatons, skirting the crater that was as big as a small mountain. In the distance, the reddening sky seemed watchful. We neared the line that for us marked the boundary between our right to live and death. Beneath our thick shells our bodies trembled all over with anguish. Nothing was changed in the empyrean of the heavens. The heartbreaking silence continued.

A few yards away we began to notice other summits similar to the one we were on. And the farther we went, the more sprang up. Now we realized that on the other side of the mountain were neither woods nor plains but merely more and more mountains all soaring toward the red sky. In this life of silence there was nothing more to hope for. The slab under our feet suddenly began to vibrate and we knew we were very close to the pulsating heart. Our own pounding hearts formed a fellowship of solitude with it. Nothing would ever again give us hope; we were no longer even tempted to live. Rather, the crater which we guessed to be the cause of all our troubles exerted a compelling fascination upon us. Toine was the first to scale the stone pass that encircled it. I was right behind him. As soon as we touched the rock we felt our fatigue fall away, as if by magic; but not our anguish. On the contrary, fed by an instinct for danger, it told us to flee as quickly as possible. In spite of it, we reached the level of the crater. Stronger than the fear that clutched us was the magnetism of the pit we peered into. A rim of stone wide enough to walk along surrounded this gaping mouth of a volcano, doubtless somnolent.

A feeling of giddiness invoked by the abyss which we sensed close at hand almost made us lose our balance. When we came to the edge of the pit my limbs trembled distressingly. Dazzled by the light, my eyes at first could not pierce the surrounding darkness of the chasm. But from the depths the sound of breathing reached us clearly, and the rhythmic beating grew more pronounced. Toine stood there, his head bent, his eyes fixed upon the void. Nothing human was left of his face. He was no more than a mirror of myself, for in him I saw what I, too, had become.

Suddenly the shoulders of my old companion collapsed as if under the impact of an enormous weight and it was then that I perceived, at the bottom of the enormous crater, the horrible thing that almost propelled me headlong into the cursed pit forever.

Floating in the middle of a lake of blood, a blue eye with an unimaginably huge black pupil stared at us. Toine screamed, and in the effort, part of his mask cracked, disfiguring for all eternity the mud-molded features.

Offering not the slightest resistance, I allowed him to lead me on. When we arrived at the external rim of the crater Toine pushed me and I rolled down a few yards to the slab of the summit. Instantly we felt engulfed by the immense fatigue we had shed earlier upon reaching the crater. Dragging ourselves a little farther toward the ledge of the platform, we let ourselves roll down the steep slope of the mountain. At first we slid at a dizzy speed, colliding on the way with statues resembling ourselves. All of us were now a mass of mineral beings sweeping down the accursed mountain. Then suddenly we stopped, as if stayed by a mysterious hand, our backs stuck to the stone, without any possibility of ever pulling loose.

The only memory that remains during the centuries of my life in stone is the gentle touch of tears on a man's face.

Gentilly, May 1963